'So, you're trying to control me, are you?'

Tina glared at him. 'Well, maybe I don't want to be controlled.'

Justin smiled an evasive smile, quite untouched by the scathing note in Tina's voice.

'No, you never did. That's what makes it so enjoyable. I'm really looking forward to having you back in my employ.'

'You mean back in your power! You're going to torment me and make my life a misery!'

'Sounds good to me.' Justin let his gaze drift over her. 'I always did enjoy tormenting you!'

There was something intensely sexual about the way he said it. And Tina found herself utterly powerless to stop herself responding.

Stephanie Howard was born and brought up in Dundee in Scotland, and educated at the London School of Economics. For ten years she worked as a journalist in London on a variety of women's magazines, among them *Woman's Own*, and was latterly editor of the now defunct *Honey*. She has spent many years living and working abroad—in Italy, Malaysia, the Philippines and in the Middle East.

Recent titles by the same author:

COME BACK FOREVER
THE BEST FOR LAST

THE MAN WHO
BROKE HEARTS

BY
STEPHANIE HOWARD

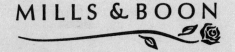

MILLS & BOON

MILLS & BOON and the Rose Device
are trademarks of the publisher.
Harlequin Mills & Boon Limited,
Eton House, 18-24 Paradise Road, Richmond, Surrey TW9 1SR
This edition published by arrangement with
Harlequin Enterprises B.V.

© Stephanie Howard 1995

ISBN 0 263 79241 2

Set in Times Roman 11 on 12 pt.
01-9510-47841 C1

Made and printed in Great Britain

CHAPTER ONE

'GOOD heavens! I'm so sorry! That was my fault.
I wasn't looking where I was going.'

As she spoke, Tina didn't even glance at her
victim—the man she'd just collided with somewhat
violently as she'd hurried across the conference-
room full of noisy fellow-journalists. All her attention was fixed on the glass of champagne
cocktail which had very nearly been sent flying out
of her hand—and most of whose contents were now
dripping down her arm.

But then her victim spoke.

'No need to apologise. It seems to me you've
come off worst.'

In an instant Tina had forgotten about her im-
promptu shower. The unexpected sound of that
deep velvety voice had instantly rooted her to the
spot. A great deal of time had passed since she'd
last heard it, but it was not a voice she was ever
likely to forget. Her heart hammering, she looked
up into Justin Marlowe's face.

'Like I said,' he repeated, smiling, 'you seem to
have come off worst.'

'Yes, I do.'

It was the only response Tina could manage. She
could barely stand for the rush of emotion that
poured through her at the sight of that arrogant

Greek god face. Suddenly, there was a tempest raging inside her. Suddenly, she was finding it difficult to breathe.

'Are you OK? You look a little stunned. You haven't hurt yourself, I trust?'

'No. I'm OK. Just a little stunned, as you say. That was quite a nasty collision.'

Tina was amazed, and relieved, at how composed and cool she sounded. She hadn't spoken to Justin Marlowe or been this close to him for three years—for, though she'd seen him from time to time at other receptions like this one, neither had ever even so much as acknowledged the other's presence. And now she was right next to him, looking into those iron-grey eyes of his that she had believed no longer had the power to affect her, and she was tumbling into an abyss of pain and confusion. In an instant her blood had turned to knives in her veins.

'I seem to have made a bit of a mess.'

Her fingers tight around her wine glass, she tore her gaze from his and glanced down, only half seeingly, at the wet splashes on her silk blouse. He was right. She had definitely come off worst in their encounter. There wasn't a mark on his immaculate navy suit. But then, she thought wryly, wasn't that always the case? Didn't she always come off worst in her encounters with Justin Marlowe?

That thought was like a splash of cold water in her face. It pulled her up abruptly. Why was she reacting so foolishly? Justin Marlowe was nothing but a cold-hearted bastard. The only emotion he should be capable of inspiring in her was dislike.

'Here. Take this.' He had reached into his trouser pocket and was pulling out a folded, spotlessly white handkerchief. He held it out to her, then, before she could protest, he had taken her wine glass and handed it to a passing waiter. 'You can use it to mop up the worst of the damage.'

Tina's foolishness had all fled in a flickering instant to be replaced by a quick keen sense of irritation. Who the devil did he think he was, taking over in this fashion? She felt tempted to tell him what to do with his handkerchief. But she let common sense prevail. She rather needed to mop up and she knew she had no tissues in her bag.

So she took the proffered handkerchief, murmuring a curt, 'Thank you,' as she did so. Then, looking up into his face again, she observed in a cutting tone, 'Whatever would I have done if you hadn't been here?'

'Well, you wouldn't have bumped into me, so you wouldn't have needed my assistance.'

Justin eyed her with those dark eyes of his that could burn holes in paper, his tone amused and lightly mocking. His gaze skimmed over her, over the long blonde hair that fell past her shoulders in platinum ripples, over the tall, model-like figure dressed in cream blouse and matching skirt, to settle on her eyes, the perfect blue of a Ming vase, which currently looked back at him with an expression as cold as porcelain.

'But don't worry, it's always a pleasure to bump into a lovely young lady.'

It was a throwaway line. Barely even a compliment. He was simply spelling out to her how he thought of her these days—unemotionally, distantly, as 'a lovely young lady'. It meant nothing to him that once they had been lovers.

It meant nothing to her either. Tina detached her gaze from his and dabbed at her wet hand with the folded handkerchief. The only thing that mattered was how much she hated him.

'So, where were you off to in such a hurry that you ended up ploughing straight into me?' As Tina glanced up at him again, Justin smiled amusedly. 'One thing's for sure—I know you didn't bump into me on purpose.'

That was true enough. As he had avoided her over the years, so Tina, equally assiduously, had avoided him. And, to be truthful, she hadn't even known he was here today. He must have only recently arrived at the reception.

Before she could answer, he added, 'One minute you were speaking to your friends, and the next you were heading towards me like a bulldozer.'

'Not heading towards you. I thought I saw someone I wanted to speak to. At the last minute I realised it wasn't her at all.'

So, Tina was thinking, he was watching me, was he? There was something a little disquieting about that.

Justin was continuing, 'I suppose you know lots of people here.' He cast a quick glance round the room in which they were standing—the conference hall of one of London's top hotels that was currently playing host to a big press reception. 'After all, you're someone pretty important these days. No less than the features editor of *Scope.*'

'Oh, not so important. Not nearly as important as yourself.'

One perfectly shaped eyebrow lifted over one porcelain-blue eye. Did he think he could mock her and get away with it? Tina wondered. Well, he was wrong if he did. No one did that any more. In the three years since their parting she had grown a little more worldly, a little more sophisticated, a little more smart. These days, with perfect poise, she could hold her own with anyone. And she could certainly hold her own with a skunk like Justin Marlowe.

Tina continued, a light, mocking smile on her lips, 'You, after all, are the owner of JM Publishing. You must own or be on the point of taking over most of the newspapers and magazines represented in this room.'

'Not quite.' Justin smiled sardonically. 'Only forty per cent. But don't worry, I'm working on the others.'

Tina did not smile back. He hasn't changed, she reflected. Still the same old overbearing self-assurance. Once, she had found that side of him exciting. She'd been stimulated and charmed by his unstoppable dynamism. But in the end she'd discovered it was really just pure selfishness. Justin Marlowe cared for no one but himself.

He hadn't changed much in the looks department either. Now that that moment of foolish turmoil had receded and she was able to look him straight in the face, Tina could see that he was just the same as ever. Perhaps there were a few more lines around the long-lashed dark grey eyes and in the corners of the passionate, well-shaped mouth— as one would expect of a man of thirty-six. But his features were still as arrestingly handsome as ever and the hair that he wore casually swept back from his forehead was still as glossily black as a raven's wing.

Still beautiful on the outside, she thought, and rotten to the core underneath.

Tina finished drying her hand and held out the handkerchief to him. 'So, is that why you're here?' Her tone was disapproving. 'On a kind of window-shopping expedition? To see what you're going to buy up next?'

Justin smiled. 'I already know what I'm going to buy up next.'

'You mean Berry's—the company I work for?'

That was the rumour that was going around. In fact, that was the very subject that Tina and her friends had been discussing with some concern just a few minutes ago, while Justin had been secretly observing them.

And talk about coincidence....! Someone 'up there' must have been listening. For Tina had been proposing that it might be a good idea if one of them were to pay a visit to JM Publishing and have a word with Justin Marlowe. For, in fact, there were

a number of rumours going around and some of
them were deeply disturbing. It seemed there was
more than just a simple take-over in the air. And
Tina was all for getting to the bottom of it.

Well, here's your chance, she told herself now.
This totally unplanned confrontation wasn't quite
what she'd had in mind, but all the same it was too
good an opportunity to miss.

'So, is that right?' she pressed him now. 'Is
Berry's next on your shopping list?'

To her surprise, he shook his head. 'Actually, I
wasn't referring to Berry's...'

As he paused, just for an instant a spark of hope
touched Tina's heart. Were these rumours they were
all so concerned about just rumours, after all? But
the hope was barely formed when Justin shattered
it.

'Berry's I consider to be already in the bag.'

He took the handkerchief, but did not return it
to his pocket.

Tina felt herself blanch. 'So, the stories are true,
then? You really are about to take over Berry's?'

'There are still a couple of papers to be signed,
but the answer is yes. I am indeed about to take
over Berry's.' At her sudden pallor he smiled the
sadistic smile of a tiger. 'You may congratulate me.
And yourself, of course. You're about to have a
new boss.'

'How unfortunate.'

Suddenly, there was a lead weight in Tina's
stomach. It grew heavier as he elaborated. 'Just like
old times, eh?'

Old times. Bad times. Tina glared at him. 'To be frank, I can't think of anything worse.' For she had worked for him in the past. That was how they'd first met. And it was an experience she had no desire to repeat.

But Justin was still smiling his sadistic tiger's smile. The smile of a tiger lazily sharpening its claws. 'I was just thinking, as I was watching you chatting to your friends there, how much I'm going to enjoy having you back under my wing.'

'Under your wing? You mean in your claws!'

And suddenly, as she glared at him, Tina felt another shiver as a new suspicion occurred to her. She hadn't bumped into him. More likely, he'd bumped into her. He'd deliberately orchestrated this encounter so that he could tell her this bad news to her face and gloat.

She fixed him with a flinty look. 'I suppose you're feeling pretty pleased?'

'Immensely pleased. However, I must say I'm saddened——' He broke off to smile a smile that was rather more triumphant than sad. 'Saddened that you unfortunately don't appear to share my pleasure.'

'No, I don't and I'm afraid neither will anyone else at Berry's. Frankly, this is the worst news you could possibly have given me. Everyone at Berry's is going to be devastated. Nobody wants you to take over the company.'

'Really?' Justin arched one caustic black eyebrow. He regarded her narrowly for a moment. 'That's extremely team-spirited of you, I must say, to care about the feelings of your colleagues.' The eyebrow lifted a little higher. 'Quite out of character.'

Tina felt a twist inside her as she remembered the episode that had given him that low, and totally unjust, opinion of her. It had been their last bitter encounter, when all she had cared about was paying back some small measure of the huge hurt he'd inflicted on her. She'd been totally out of her mind that day.

But she would never take back the things she had said to him. She knew they'd done no more than slightly bruise his ego, but even that was a source of some satisfaction. And she didn't give a damn what he thought of her anyway.

She tilted her chin at him and totally ignored his comment. 'Everyone, on all the magazines at Berry's, is very much against you,' she repeated.

'Are they?' He looked as concerned as an elephant with a fleabite. 'Don't worry, they'll learn to love me. Everybody does.'

He said it so flippantly, yet looking straight at her, as though he had meant it as a callous reminder of the overpowering love he had once aroused in her.

Tina felt herself recoil. Her heart thudded inside her. 'If they do, they soon get over it,' she shot back at him in a harsh tone. 'It's not the kind of love that runs very deep.'

That was what she had wanted him to believe of her three years ago. It was why she'd said the things she'd said at their last meeting. She'd had too much pride to let him see her bruised, bleeding heart.

And it seemed she'd done a good job. He flicked a look back at her now. 'But some people are only capable of the shallowest emotions. They just take what they can get and then cynically move on.'

Then he smiled, his eyes darkening, and let his gaze travel over her. 'The heart of a vampire in the body of an angel,' he purred.

This was nothing like the way he had looked at her earlier. Then his gaze had been perfunctory and mocking. But now his eyes lingered, moving like touching fingers, caressing the full, generous curves of her breasts, the dip of her waist, the gentle flare of her hips. And it was a far too familiar scrutiny. Far too knowing. His eyes held the arrogant look of a man taking a stroll over territory he had once known very well.

How dared he? Bristling with anger, Tina opened her mouth to rebuke him. But before she could utter a word she was suddenly freezing to the spot.

For he was reaching out towards her with the handkerchief. 'You've missed a bit here,' he was saying in an amused tone as he dabbed lightly at the lapel of her cream silk blouse. Then as she tried to move he caught her lightly by the arm. 'Stand still. How can I see what I'm doing if you move?'

A rush of panic seized her. All at once she had difficulty breathing. It was crazy; they were in a public place, surrounded by people, yet all at once Tina felt like a helpless prisoner. The hand that gripped her arm was like a manacle holding her. A manacle of red-hot burning steel.

'You don't need to do that!'

'It's no trouble, I assure you.'

'No, really... But really...'

Her heart was jumping inside her. For not only was he holding her, not only was he touching her, but, much worse, all at once she had suddenly become aware of the light scent of the handkerchief that drifted up to her nostrils.

It was his scent. That cool, clean scent she remembered. And suddenly, like some magic carpet of the senses, it was transporting her back to that time three years ago when she had been as familiar with that scent as with the scent of her own body.

And suddenly, in her mind she was lying naked beside him, caressing him, touching him, pressing against him, dizzy and drunk with desire and love for him.

It was a shattering moment. She felt something crumble inside her as she glanced up, helplessly, into the arrogant dark eyes that looked down on her now, distant and uncaring. For a moment her heart seemed to break all over again. A sense of paralysing loss went flooding through her.

'There, that's better.' Justin was stepping away now, releasing his grip on her arm as he did so. Then he handed her the handkerchief. 'There's another spot on the collar. But perhaps I'd better let you attend to that.'

He was mocking her. He had picked up her sudden anguish and it appealed to his sadistic sense of humour. Perhaps, she thought wretchedly, he'd done it on purpose, guessing in advance how she would react. It still amused him to play with her, even after all these years.

At that thought Tina's anguish turned instantly to anger. She was not his plaything—though he had once treated her as though she were. She was a twenty-five-year-old woman whom no other man in the world would ever have dared to treat so familiarly. And all he was to her was a man she despised with all her heart.

She took a pointed step away from him, her blue eyes chipped porcelain. 'It's not like you to be so solicitous,' she observed frostily. 'And I can assure you I neither need nor want your help in any way.'

'But it's my pleasure.' Justin simply smiled in the face of her annoyance. 'As I said before, you're someone pretty important these days. One feels obliged to offer one's services.' A sarcastic look touched his eyes. 'Though I wasn't doing you full justice when I referred to you earlier as features editor of *Scope*. I understand that these days you're also acting editor.'

'Only while Maggie's ill.' Maggie was *Scope*'s editor. 'It's only a temporary position.'

'But one that could lead to greater glory in the future. If you do a good job, who knows what it could lead to—especially with Maggie due to retire in a couple of years?'

Tina was well aware of that and to anyone else she would have admitted it. But not to Justin. He would only twist it.

She told him, deadpan. 'I don't expect it to lead to anything. Maggie will be back at her desk in a couple of weeks.'

'She's got some stomach trouble, I hear.'

'Yes, but nothing serious.'

'So, you didn't put arsenic in her tea, after all?' As Tina scowled at him, Justin added, 'I wouldn't put it past you. Remember, I know how ambitious you are. And you're not one to let loyalty or scruples get in your way. No wonder you've made such a rapid rise to the top.'

Tina resented that, though, of course, she knew why he'd said it. It was all part of the lie she'd fed him three years ago.

She straightened a little, tilted her chin and defended herself. 'I've got where I am because I've worked hard,' she informed him.

'Yes, I'm sure you have. Single-mindedly and unstintingly.' Then he smiled unexpectedly and surprised her as he added, 'Besides, you have talent.' His hard expression softened. 'And I take pride in having been one of the first to recognise it.'

Tina had to hold back a blush as a rush of remembrance poured through her. For it was true; he'd been one of the first to show faith in her. And she'd have felt grateful to him for that if what had happened later hadn't happened. But the pain he had caused her later cancelled all gratitude out.

She looked back at him, breathing carefully, hiding her emotions. 'That,' she told him quietly, 'was a long time ago.'

'Indeed it was. You were young and innocent then.' He smiled a cynical smile. 'Or at least I thought you were.'

'I was innocent until I met you.'

She wished she hadn't said that. It made her sound like an undone virgin, and that wasn't the accusation she'd wanted to make. For it was not the taking of her sexual innocence that Tina resented, but the destruction of another kind of innocence. He had totally betrayed her trust.

All the time he'd been with her, seducing her and making her fall for him, he had secretly been involved with another woman. A woman Tina had known well. Her immediate boss at JM Publishing. The flaming redhead she and her friends had dubbed the Red Dragon.

And worse. He had even asked the Red Dragon to be his wife.

Remembering, Tina was aware of a plummeting within her. Just for an instant, all the heartbreak of that betrayal was tearing inside her, vivid and real again. For that had been the worst time of her life.

But it was all in the past now. Past and forgotten. She had long stopped caring about Justin and the Red Dragon, the eternally engaged couple, for they still hadn't married.

She thinned her lips at him. 'You showed me the ways of the world. The seamier ways of the world, that is.'

'Oh, I suspect you already knew them. You probably even invented a few of them. And you've

probably invented a few more in the meantime.
After all, look how well you've flourished.'

He was quite without remorse, but then he always
had been. He had never once apologised for the
terrible thing he'd done to her.

But Tina shrugged that off. Hadn't he, in truth,
done her a favour? For after her break-up with
Justin she'd banished love from her heart and de-
dicated herself body and soul to her career. Her
work had kept her sane, and without that dedi-
cation she would probably never have risen up the
ladder so fast.

She hadn't risen as fast as Justin, though. His
rise had been spectacular. Over the past three years
JM Publishing had mushroomed. He'd been taking
over publishing houses left, right and centre, until
these days his greedy wings spread halfway across
the globe.

Narrowing her eyes, she observed disparagingly,
'Judging by the little empire you've built for
yourself, I'd say you were the one who knows how
to flourish.'

'Then you should be glad I'm taking you over.
If I flourish, Berry's will flourish too.'

'We'd prefer to flourish on our own, thanks.'

'But you're not flourishing, are you? Left on your
own, the company will fold within the year.'

'That's absolute rubbish!' Tina's blue eyes
flashed dismissively. She'd heard Berry's was in
trouble, but things weren't *that* bad. 'I know some
of Berry's magazines are losing money. But not all
of them are. I know *Scope* isn't, for a fact.'

'No, it isn't. It's doing rather well. The only one that is.'

'So, you see, we could survive very well without you.'

'We? You mean *Scope*. The others would go under.' The dark eyes narrowed and seemed to hook into her face. 'But you don't care about that, do you? You only care about yourself.'

This time Tina retaliated. 'You couldn't be further from the truth. What I want is for *all* of Berry's magazines to survive—which they won't, for sure, if you get your hands on them!'

Eyes sparking, she accused him, 'You talk so high and mighty, but I know what's really at the back of this take-over. You want to take over Berry's just so you can get your hands on *Scope*. We're doing too well for your comfort, aren't we?'

'And what is that supposed to mean?'

Faker! He knew what she meant! For Tina was suddenly absolutely certain that all the other dreadful rumours she'd been hearing were true too. There was a lot more in the air than just a simple take-over. But if he wanted to play dumb, she'd be only to happy to explain.

'We're too much competition for *Miranda* these days. *Miranda*'s losing readers to us. Everybody knows it. And you don't like that. That's why you want to buy us—so you can merge *Scope* with *Miranda* and keep your precious flagship afloat!'

And keep your precious fiancée in a job, she might have added. For his fiancée, the Red Dragon, was the editor of *Miranda*.

Justin paused for an instant, as though he might deny the accusation. Then a slow, callous smile spread over his face.

'Well, naturally I would want to keep *Miranda* afloat. And naturally I'll take whatever measures are required, no matter how unpalatable they may be to some.'

'So, you are going to fold *Scope*?'

'You'll find out in good time.' He paused and fixed her with eyes of granite. 'So, you're admitting it at last. All you're really worried about's your own job.'

Tina's cheeks had grown pale. All her worst fears were confirmed. The magazine she loved and had poured her life into was about to be ruthlessly sacrificed.

And it wasn't fair! All at once, she was trembling with fury.

'Of course I'm worried about my job. I'd be a liar if I denied it.' Tina spoke softly—after all, they were in a public place—yet every taut syllable seethed with outrage. 'But my first concern is *Scope*. It's a good magazine. It's an *excellent* magazine. A leader in its field. How can you do this?' Her voice was cracking with emotion as she searched his eyes in vain for some spark of compassion. 'Can't you see that *Scope* is special? It doesn't deserve to be sacrificed just to please you and your——'

For some reason she faltered, the word sticking in her throat.

She saw Justin smile. 'Me and my what?'

It was the smile that did it. Something snapped inside her.

'You and that bitch of a fiancée of yours!' she spat.

Tina was mortified. All she'd meant to say was fiancée. The bitch bit had somehow come tumbling out on its own.

As she stood there, pale-faced, Justin watched her for a moment as though she were some crawly thing that had just escaped from behind a rock. Then, detaching his eyes, he glanced at his watch.

'I'm afraid I have to go now. I have an empire to run. But if not a pleasure, at least it's been most illuminating bumping into you.'

He started to turn away, then he paused and fixed his eyes on her face again.

'I knew I was going to enjoy working alongside you again, but until this moment I hadn't realised quite how much.' He smiled his tiger's smile again. 'What was that phrase you used earlier? Having you in my claws, I believe, was how you put it. Yes, I can tell I'm going to enjoy that very much.'

Then, before she could say a word, he was turning on his heel and disappearing swiftly off through the crowd.

Tina watched him go through eyes that could barely focus, feeling seasick with the horror that poured through her in great waves. Though it wasn't Justin's warning that filled her with horror. It was her own spiteful outburst against his fiancée.

That had taken her by surprise. It had genuinely shocked her. Usually, she just made jokes about the Red Dragon. But a moment ago she definitely hadn't been joking. There'd been real anger, real dislike, real resentment in her heart against the woman who, three years ago, had stolen the man she loved. There'd been the kind of pain she'd believed she'd put behind her long ago.

She shivered. To know that pain still lurked inside her, ready to scrape at any moment like a dagger against her heart, filled her with a fear that was far more terrible than the fear of anything that Justin could do to her.

Although as she stared after him she was aware that that scared her too. What terrible, evil revenge was he planning?

CHAPTER TWO

IT WAS only after Justin had gone and Tina had recovered her senses that she realised she was still holding his handkerchief in her hand. She shoved it in her bag, resisting the urge to chuck it in some corner. One thing she definitely wouldn't do was run after him to return it!

Back home at the end of the day she deposited it in the washing machine, handling it at arm's length, as though it might bite her. And that was where it still was as she sat at her office desk next morning, struggling to concentrate on the manuscript before her. Though it was hard. Her mind kept skipping back to yesterday's encounter with Justin.

It had tormented her all night. She'd scarcely slept a wink for the horror she still felt at her shameful outburst against his fiancée.

What on earth had provoked it? Where had these long-dead feelings come from? The pain, the anger, the sense of loss, the resentment? She didn't care any more that she'd lost Justin to the Red Dragon. Losing Justin, she'd come to realise, had been a lucky escape. So what on earth had caused her to react like that?

Some kind of madness, she'd decided. That mocking smile he'd smiled at her had thrown her back to that moment three years ago when she'd discovered that the man she'd believed was in love with her had just got engaged to another woman.

The Red Dragon, when she'd broken the news to her, had smiled a smile like that.

Tina clenched her teeth now and scowled down at the manuscript before her. But all that was ancient history and she'd long since got over it. As far as she was concerned, the Red Dragon was welcome to him. She and Justin could marry any time they liked.

In fact, the sooner the better. For Tina it would be a relief. It would finally draw a line beneath the entire messy episode.

'Hi there! How's my favourite acting editor?'

Tina started and glanced up as a voice broke through her reverie. Then she smiled at the wiry, leather-jacketed figure who was grinning down at her from the other side of her desk.

'Hi, Mike.' As always, she was delighted to see him. Mike Laing was one of the top fashion photographers in London and he also happened to be a very good friend.

She leaned back in her seat and pulled a wry face as she gestured at the pile of work on her desk— manuscripts, letters, transparencies, proofs, all urgently waiting to be dealt with.

'Right now your favourite acting editor's feeling a bit frazzled,' she confessed.

'Well, she doesn't look it.' Mike seated himself on the edge of the desk. 'She's looking as serenely beautiful as ever.'

Then as Tina smiled and shook her head—her standard response to Mike's compliments—he enquired sympathetically, 'Overworking you, are they?'

'Not really.'

Tina ran a hand through her silky blonde hair. She was doing two jobs these days, but that didn't bother her. In fact, to tell the truth, she relished the challenge, and she'd been coping perfectly till thoughts of Justin had come to torment her! However, there was one problem, as she explained now to Mike.

'One of my regular freelances has let me down rather badly. She's handed in this article that's a total disaster. I can't understand it. She's generally so reliable.' She cast an irritated glance at the manuscript she'd been working on. 'It's going to take me hours to pull this gibberish into shape.'

'Throw it back at her. Get her to redo it.'

'I would, only she's not here. She's out of the country. She's gone off to France or somewhere on an assignment for some other magazine. And she was late handing this in. The printers need it by Monday. I've got no choice, I'm afraid. I've got to do it myself.'

Mike pulled a sympathetic face, then he winked and leaned towards her. 'I reckon you deserve a treat for working so hard. Let me take you out for a drink after work.'

'I wish I could, Mike——'

'I've discovered this great new wine bar,' he cut in quickly before she could say 'but'. 'The food's terrific and they play great jazz.'

But Tina smiled and shook her head. 'I really can't, Mike. I'm going to be stuck at my desk till late.'

Mike looked disappointed, but he didn't push her. He never did. He knew it got him nowhere. Just like all the other men in Tina's life these days, he knew he would never be more than just a friend.

For Tina had become an expert at keeping men at a distance. Sometimes it surprised her how easily she did it. Maybe I'm turning into a bit of a dragon myself, she'd sometimes thought. For just one cool warning flicker from those china-blue eyes of hers and they got the message loud and clear.

But, dragon or not, that was the way she wanted it. No mess. No entanglements. No more broken hearts. Maybe one day—though only maybe— things would be different, but for now where her heart belonged was in her work.

Mike proceeded to change the subject now, regarding her with interest. 'Hey, your chief sub-editor's just been telling me that you collared Justin Marlowe at the reception yesterday. What did he have to say for himself?'

Tina felt a jolt inside her at the mention of Justin's name. Over the past couple of minutes she'd actually managed not to think of him, but here he was springing out of the shadows to torment her again!

'So, Vicki told you, did she?' Tina smiled a small smile. Vicki, *Scope*'s chief sub, had been with her at the reception yesterday and she'd been telling everyone about Tina's encounter with Justin Marlowe—even though, Tina reflected, she didn't know the half of it!

'Well, she probably also told you that the news isn't good. If this take-over goes ahead, *Scope* will go under. He plans to merge us with *Miranda*.'

Mike looked surprised. 'Did he actually say that?'

'More or less.' Tina pulled a wry face. 'I'm afraid you were wrong and I was right.'

In the past, Mike had frequently expressed the opinion that it might not be a bad thing if JM Publishing took over Berry's. He was an enthusiastic admirer of Justin's thrusting young company—and not just because JM gave him a lot of work! 'They know how to make money and keep up standards,' he'd often said.

But his opinion about the take-over was totally misguided, as Tina had constantly argued over the weeks. She told him now, 'Somehow, Marlowe's got to be stopped.'

'If you're right, yes, he has. That would be a disaster.' Mike frowned. 'But I can't understand why he would do that. It doesn't make sense. *Scope*'s a successful magazine.' Then he shrugged. 'Maybe business-wise his judgement's a little impaired these days. I understand he's got other things on his mind.'

Tina was instantly curious. 'Like what?' she demanded.

But at that moment they were interrupted as Sasha, *Scope*'s fashion editor, stuck her brightly hennaed head round the office door.

'Excuse me.' She smiled at Tina. Then she turned to Mike. 'Ready when you are with those transparencies.'

Mike started to stand up. 'I'll be right with you.' Then he winked down at Tina. 'I'll leave you to get on with your work.'

But Tina was no longer thinking of work. She narrowed her blue eyes at him. 'What did you mean when you said Justin Marlowe had other things on his mind?'

'Haven't you heard?' Mike was heading for the door. 'He and the Red Dragon are finally about to get spliced. The word is she's been out scouring Bond Street for a wedding-dress. It looks as though she's finally bagged him after all these years.'

'Good luck to her.'

Tina said it as though she really meant it and her gaze was perfectly steady as she watched Mike disappear out through the door. And she did mean it. Surely? Hadn't she just been thinking that it would be a relief when Justin and the Red Dragon finally married?

But as she sat frozen in her chair she was aware that she'd stopped breathing and that her stomach had suddenly turned to lead.

Tina remained at her desk that night until well after seven, but by then there was no point in staying on any longer. She'd done all the work she could for now on the faulty manuscript, though it definitely still wasn't up to scratch.

She pushed it aside wearily. She'd have to fix up another interview to fill in the gaps and give it a bit more substance. And that would probably mean a trip to the Cotswolds over the weekend. She tossed down her pen. But for tonight she was through.

But she still didn't make a move. She sat staring into space and let her mind roam over the subject she had kept shut out for the past few hours. Justin and the Red Dragon. And the long-threatened wedding. So, it was actually about to happen after all.

She'd got over the stupid paralysis that had struck her on first hearing the news. And heaven knew why it had shocked her anyway. She felt composed now and genuinely glad that it was about to happen. This was the final line in the final chapter. At last she'd be able to close the book.

At that thought she felt a wry smile touch her lips. Chapter one had promised a very different ending. Who ever would have guessed then that things would turn out the way they had?

Tina had been twenty-one years old, fresh out of college and as keen as mustard to make a name for herself in journalism when she had joined *Miranda* as a sub-editor nearly five years ago.

As she'd told her new boss at the interview, 'It's always been my dream to work in magazines. There's nothing else I've ever wanted to do.'

Her new boss had been a woman nearly ten years her senior, a tall, stunning redhead with the reed-thin figure of a model and a wardrobe that came straight out of the pages of her own glossy magazine. Her name was Eunice Robinson and though Tina had guessed even then that she probably had a temperament to match her hair she'd had no idea that she'd end up dubbing her the Red Dragon!

On the contrary, she'd been excited at the prospect of joining Eunice's team. On the phone to her parents when she'd been offered the job, she'd confided, 'The atmosphere's so professional and high-powered and sophisticated. I'm going to learn so much. I can't wait to get started!'

And so she'd dived in, full of enthusiasm.

Her first encounter with Justin Marlowe had come in her second week at JM Publishing.

'Come in. Sit down. Make yourself comfortable,' he'd told her as his secretary showed Tina into his office. He'd held out his hand to her. 'I'm Justin Marlowe. Welcome to JM Publishing. How are you settling in?'

Tina had taken his hand and looked into his face, feeling a shiver of awareness like electric fingers down her spine. The other sub-editors had told her about Justin Marlowe and that he was the dishiest man on the face of the planet. But he was more than just dishy, she'd decided instantly. This man had a special kind of magic.

She'd felt a ripple of innocent pleasure as he'd shaken her hand and smiled at her. Boy, I'm lucky! she'd thought. Not only have I just succeeded in landing my dream job, I've also got the hand-somest boss!

Smiling back at him, she told him, 'I'm settling in very well, thanks. I'm sure I'm going to love it here.' Her eyes glowed keenly as she added, 'I think *Miranda*'s a wonderful magazine.'

'So do we and I'm very glad to hear that you agree.' The iron-grey eyes, which she would later discover could at times look as cold as the North Sea in winter, twinkled warmly at her enthusiasm. 'I suspect you're going to be a most valuable ad-dition to the team.'

'Oh, I hope so. I really hope so. I'll do my best.'

Justin Marlowe smiled. 'Then you're halfway there.' He leaned back a little in his leather button-back chair. 'So, tell me about your ambitions, Tina. Where do you see yourself in five years' time?'

'Still on *Miranda*, I hope.' She blushed a little. How truthful, she wondered, did he really expect her to be? For she really did have high ambitions.

He sensed her ambivalence. 'Go on,' he urged her. 'You can tell me. We encourage ambition in this company.'

Tina took a deep breath and decided to take him at his word. 'Well, first I want to learn to be a good sub-editor, but I also want to do a bit of writing. I love writing. I want to do articles on anything and everything.'

Then, as he nodded encouragingly, she decided to bare her soul. 'And one day what I'd really like is to be an editor.'

'An editor, eh? Aiming for the top.' Justin nodded his dark head approvingly in response. Then he winked across at her almost conspiratorially. 'We'd better not tell Eunice. I don't think she's quite ready to retire yet.'

Tina felt herself flush crimson. 'Oh, I didn't mean that! I didn't mean editor of *Miranda*! Some other magazine. Some time in the future. A long time in the future,' she plunged on in embarrassment.

Oh, lord! she was thinking. Talk about putting your foot in it!

But Justin, if anything, seemed to approve of her revelation.

'Never apologise for your ambitions,' he told her straightforwardly. 'We encourage ambitious people at JM Publishing—as long as you have the talent to match the ambition, of course.' He smiled at her. 'And we'll soon find out if you do.'

Tina left his office feeling the world was hers to conquer. I'll show him I have talent! I'll show him how good I am! I'll show him I have it in me to achieve all my goals! she vowed.

And, over the next few months, that was precisely what she did.

Tina worked like a madwoman, loving every minute. Pretty soon she became a first-class sub-editor, renowned for her precision and witty, attention-grabbing titles. And pretty soon, too, she had a couple of short articles published. And Justin wasn't slow to acknowledge her progress.

He appeared in the office one day and stopped by her desk. 'I thought you might like to have a go at this,' he suggested, dropping an invitation on her desk. 'Have a word with Eunice. I think it might be worth a full-length interview.'

'Oh, thank you!' Tina's eyes widened as she looked down at the invitation to meet an up-and-coming young actor who'd recently been taking the British film world by storm. She looked up at Justin gratefully. 'I'll make a good job of it. I promise.'

And she made an excellent job of it. Even Eunice agreed on that and gave her piece a four-page colour double spread, with a prominent byline as the icing on the cake. Tina was over the moon with delight.

She phoned her parents in Shropshire. 'I'm sending you a couple of copies. Your daughter's a proper journalist at last!'

There was just one tiny fly in the ointment, however, as, with Justin's encouragement and guidance, Tina proceeded to move from success to success. And that fly in the ointment was the red-haired Eunice.

Tina had rapidly realised that she could be a difficult woman to work with, much given to furious outbursts when anyone displeased her. Tina had escaped her wrath at first. She'd just kept her head down and worked hard. But more and more she was finding herself in the firing line.

'These pages are late, you stupid girl!' Twice in one week Eunice stormed the accusation at her when the pages, in fact, were not late at all. 'Instead of trying to be the star of the editorial department, you'd do better to keep your mind on what you're paid for!'

That was unfair and uncalled for. Tina knew her responsibilities and always put her sub-editing duties first—though, to be truthful, the accusation had not surprised her. She'd been aware for some time that, far from wishing to encourage her, Eunice would rather like to clip her wings.

But she kept that to herself and confined herself to pointing out, 'I think if you check your diary you'll find the pages are dead on time.' Unlike some members of staff, she wasn't afraid to stand up for herself. 'Just as they always are,' she added firmly, but respectfully, simply ignoring the fulminating black look that that provoked.

For Eunice's increasingly frequent attacks were not anything Tina couldn't handle. In fact, to be truthful, they barely registered. Because suddenly something much more exciting was occupying her mind.

Justin. For something was happening between them.

It had all started with an unexpected invitation to lunch at London's Dorchester Hotel on fashionable Park Lane.

'It's part treat and part work,' Justin had told her when he'd invited her. 'We're to be the guests of a group of major travel agents and naturally I'll expect you to write a small piece for *Miranda*. But only a very small piece, so just relax and enjoy yourself. You've been working hard. You deserve a treat.'

Tina's workmates had been almost as excited as she was. 'You're obviously in the good books,' one of them had observed admiringly. 'He only issues these special invitations when he's really pleased with someone.' Then she'd pulled a mock-scowl and poked Tina in the ribs. 'I hate you, Tina Gordon, you lucky devil!'

Tina struggled to appear cool in the face of this development. The invitation was purely professional, she told herself. And certainly nothing to get all het up about.

But she was het up. She could barely see straight at the thought of it. Lunch with Justin Marlowe! The very idea made her breathless!

For, though she'd admitted it to no one, the truth of the matter was that over the six months or so she'd been at JM Publishing she'd really rather fallen for her magnetic, handsome boss. Which hardly made her unusual. Every woman he met fell for him. The entire female staff of JM Publishing was hopelessly in love with Justin Marlowe, so why should she be any different?

Yet what she felt for him *was* different. In her heart Tina was sure of it. Hers was no swooning, giggling admiration. She couldn't quite define them, but the feelings he let loose in her seemed to reach down to the very roots of her being. And sometimes it scared her. She'd never felt this way before.

Still, she was holding on very tightly to her emotions when they set off together in the company limo. Just don't make a fool of yourself, she warned herself firmly. You mean nothing to him. He's just being nice, that's all.

But nice like Justin could be nice was something Tina had never before encountered. She was only a junior employee, but he treated her like a princess, putting her at ease with that wonderful charm of his, chatting to her and looking after her as though they were on a real date. When they finally left the Dorchester just over three hours later, Tina was feeling as though she must have died and gone to heaven.

'Did you enjoy yourself?' he asked her as they climbed back into the Bentley.

'Oh, yes. It was wonderful. I mean, wonderfully interesting.'

Had he any idea, she wondered helplessly, how her heart was soaring? She'd been on plenty of very pleasant dates in the past with perfectly acceptable young men, but the past three hours with Justin had been a revelation. She'd had no idea she was capable of feeling such ecstasy. She was floating so high, she feared she might never come down again.

Justin was smiling at her. 'I enjoyed it too. Perhaps we can do it again some time?'

'Oh, yes. That would be nice.'

'Perhaps when I get back from Germany? I'm going there on business. I'll be away till the end of the week.' He smiled. 'I presume your home number's in the office files. I'll give you a ring and we can fix up something when I get back.'

'OK. If you like.'

Tina flushed to her hair roots, totally confused now, not knowing what to think. Was this a real date he was proposing? Was he really serious? If she dared to hope, would she be in for a huge disappointment?

She decided she probably would be, but she went ahead and hoped anyway. She was quite incapable of doing anything else.

Waiting for the week to pass was the finest kind of torture. At home, every time the phone rang Tina nearly shot through the ceiling. But she made herself a promise. If he didn't phone by Saturday lunchtime, she'd call up her friends and make other arrangements for the weekend. It would be masochistic madness to spend it waiting by the phone!

But on Friday evening when she got back to her flat from work the phone was ringing in the hallway.

Breathlessly, Tina grabbed it. 'Hello?' she demanded squeakily, not quite managing the cool tone she'd been aiming for. It can't be him, she was thinking, feeling her heart was about to explode.

But it was him.

'Hi, Tina. I just got back. How've you been?'

At the sound of the deep tones, Tina had to sit down. 'I'm fine.' She was burning from her scalp to her toes. 'H-how was your trip to Germany?' she stuttered.

'It went off very well, thanks.' He paused for an instant. 'How about if I tell you all about it over dinner this evening?'

'This evening?' The room was swimming round her ears. Could she believe what she was hearing or had she gone mad?

'Unless you've got something else fixed, of course...?'

He sounded disappointed. Tina rushed in to assure him, 'No, I don't have anything fixed at all.'

'Then I'll pick you up about eight. How does that sound?'

Like a dream come true, she thought. 'It sounds fine,' she said.

'Eight o'clock it is. I'll see you then. Bye for now.'

Tina was shaking so badly as she laid down the phone that she fancied she could hear the bones rattling in her fingers. For a full thirty seconds she just sat where she was, grinning like an idiot and glowing with excitement. Then with a whoop of delight she leapt to her feet, rushed through to her bedroom and flung open the cupboard doors. What on earth was she going to wear?

Justin was every bit as punctual as she'd expected he would be. At the stroke of eight o'clock his gleaming white Mercedes appeared like a fairy-tale coach and horses outside her modest red-brick flat block.

'You look terrific,' he told her as he held open the passenger door for her and she slid a little shyly into the leather-upholstered seat. 'But then you always look terrific. You're just looking particularly so tonight.'

Tina might very well have answered, So are you, but she bit her lip and just smiled at him instead. She was feeling far too nervous to pull off remarks like that!

All the same, it was true—if such a thing was actually possible! He *was* looking even more terrific than usual.

He was wearing a dark blue suit whose simple clean-cut lines showed off to perfection his manly proportions—the strong, broad shoulders, the lean hips and long legs. And the plain white shirt provided a perfect dramatic contrast to his suntanned skin and the ebony darkness of his hair.

He was a positive feast for the eyes, Tina decided. She wouldn't need to eat; she could just sit and admire him!

Justin took her to a restaurant in the heart of Mayfair. The most elegant place she'd ever set foot in. You could almost smell the gold credit cards and hear the rustle of designer labels. She was rather glad she'd worn the most stunning outfit in her wardrobe—a chic, long-skirted dress in bright cherry-red.

'Champagne,' Justin told the waiter as they were shown to their table. Then he smiled at Tina. 'Unless you'd prefer something else, of course?'

'Oh, no. Champagne's fine.'

She could hardly keep her face straight. Was this really happening or was it all a dream? Would she wake up and find herself in her local Wimpy bar with Vicki?

But at least she was rapidly losing her nervousness. There was just something about being with Justin that felt easy and right. The conversation flowed. There was no sense of strain. As they were being served their first course, she took the initiative and asked him, 'So tell me about your trip to Germany.'

But Justin shook his head. 'That was just business. Very boring.' He smiled that smile that made her heart keel over. 'What I really want to talk about this evening is you. I want you to tell me all about yourself, Tina Gordon.'

'Me? There's not much to tell. I'm just an ordinary girl from Shropshire.' Tina's cheeks had turned the same cherry-red as her dress. 'My parents both work at a local car plant and I have two sisters, one married and one at college, studying French.'

She laughed a little nervously. 'There! You have it in a nutshell!' Surely, she was thinking, he couldn't really be interested?

But it seemed she was wrong. He was shaking his head at her. 'Ah, but I don't want it in a nutshell. I want to hear all the gory details. By the end of this meal I want to know all there is to know about you.'

He meant it, too. He plied her with questions, and Tina found herself very happily opening up to him. He wasn't just being curious. He seemed genuinely interested. Flushed with pleasure, she virtually told him her life story.

She told him about her schooldays back in Shrewsbury, about the friends she grew up with and all the places she knew. She told him about the articles she used to write for the school magazine, about her ambition to work on a national magazine one day and about her wonderful parents who'd encouraged her all the way.

'You're an interesting girl.' Justin smiled at her across the table as he poured them both more wine and finished off his fillet steak—for by now they'd been talking for more than an hour. 'I knew you would be. You've got that spark in your eyes.'

Tina smiled back at him as she took a sip of her Beaujolais. 'But that's enough about me. It's your turn now,' she told him. 'Tell me something about Justin Marlowe.'

'OK. What do you want to know?'

'Everything! Fair's fair,' she laughed. 'After all, I've told you virtually everything there is to know about me!'

And so over the next hour, until coffee, Justin told her about himself. He told her about his own modest upbringing in London and about how he started his first publishing venture with a loan from a wealthy uncle.

'I owe it all to him,' he told her, 'and I'll always be grateful. I would never have made it without his help.'

'Oh, I'll bet you would.' Tina shook her blonde head at him. 'It might have taken you a little longer, but I bet you'd have made it.'

For there was one thing she had no doubts about—Justin was one of life's natural winners.

He didn't exactly dispute it, but with a serious smile he pointed out, 'A helping hand at the right time can be a great bonus, however. One must always remember to be grateful for such things.'

The remark, Tina sensed, had not in any way been intended as a reminder of the helping hand he'd given her in her career, and to have expressed her gratitude at that moment would only have embarrassed him. So she said nothing. She would thank him properly when the time was right. Besides, right now she wanted to hear more about him.

She looked into the iron-grey eyes. 'So, what are your plans for the future? JM Publishing has four successful magazines at the moment, but I get the impression you don't intend stopping there.'

He smiled. 'I'd like to expand a bit. Like you, I'm ambitious.' Then, as she laughed at that, he leaned towards her suddenly and surprised her as he added, his tone suddenly grown serious. 'But right now it's the more immediate future I'm thinking of. I'm rather hoping you'll agree to have dinner with me again tomorrow.'

Tina's heart had stopped stone-dead. Secretly, she'd been wondering what, if anything, would happen next. I couldn't bear it, she'd been thinking, if this turned out to be a one-off.

She nodded now with all the restraint she could muster. 'I'd love to have dinner with you again tomorrow.'

In fact, they spent virtually the entire weekend together. The theatre and dinner on Saturday. Lunch on Sunday, followed by a romantic walk in

Hyde Park. Then dinner together at Justin's sump-
tuous Kensington flat.

And it was on the Sunday evening, after that
candlelit dinner, that Tina knew for certain that she
was on the brink of something special. For that was
when, for very first time, he kissed her.

Tina had dreamed of that first kiss, but the reality was better.

They were sitting together on the huge, soft sofa,
two untouched cups of coffee on the low table
before them, and the atmosphere between them was
electric. It had been building up all evening. Every
smile, every glance, as the evening wore on, had
seemed to crackle with promise.

As he had led her to the sofa, Tina had scarcely
been breathing. Her heart had felt as big as a
football in her chest. It had been a relief to sit down,
her legs felt so weak.

He had laid the coffee-cups on the table and now
he was watching her, those long-lashed dark eyes
of his like molten metal against her skin.

And she was suddenly afraid to meet them.
Afraid of what her own eyes would reveal to him.
With a darting, nervous movement she reached out
to take her coffee-cup.

But her hand never reached it. He caught hold
of it in his.

'No,' he was saying, 'there's something I want
to do first.'

Then he was turning her round very gently to
face him, and suddenly his eyes were pouring into
her as his arm slipped round her waist and he drew

her closer to deliver the kiss that had been waiting all evening to happen.

Tina was already hyped up, but at the moment his lips touched hers a jolt of excitement, so huge and so powerful that even in her wildest moments she could never have imagined it, went jackknifing through her, leaving her throbbing and breathless, her senses reeling, her head in a spin.

Never had a kiss been more worth waiting for. Tina clung to him as a bushfire went rampaging through her, melting her bones, sending flames shooting from her skin. Hungrily, she kissed him back, her lips as eager as his.

After a while, the tempest within them abated a little. Wrapped in each other's arms, they sat together amid the tumbled cushions, quietly, the only sound the furious pounding of their two hearts.

'You're a very special girl.' Justin's hands caressed her. 'I hope we're going to see a very great deal of each other in the future.'

Tina shuddered beneath his touch, loving the cool, masterful touch of him, drinking in the delicious scent of him through hungry nostrils.

'I hope so too,' she murmured. 'I hope so very much.'

He kissed her eyes, her lips, her chin, her forehead, then paused for a moment to press his lips lingeringly against the warm, throbbing pulse in the hollow of her throat.

'There's just one thing,' he murmured softly, glancing up at her. He hesitated for an instant. 'I think we ought to be discreet.'

Tina had already been thinking that. She nodded and smiled at him. 'You're right.' She had no desire to start tongues wagging around the office. 'I won't breathe a word to a soul,' she agreed.

'Good girl.' Justin held her close for a moment. Then he looked down at her, his dark eyes bright with emotion. 'I think what lies ahead of us is going to be very special indeed.'

It was. The next nine months were the happiest of Tina's life. Her romance with Justin seemed to go from strength to strength. He was busy a lot of the time and he travelled a great deal, presiding over his growing empire, and there were few more weekends spent entirely together like that first one, though they spent all the time they could together.

When she didn't see him, Tina pined for him. Being without him was awful. For with every day that passed she was falling more deeply in love with him, with a love that brightened every corner of her life. She was so in love she scarcely cared about Eunice's ever more frequent tantrums at the office. Justin had declared his love for her. She could take anything in her stride.

Besides, these days, her career took second place in her heart. What drove her and gave her life meaning was her love for Justin.

And then, just as she was growing used to her state of happiness, the bubble burst; she learned the truth and was sent crashing down like a spent meteorite to earth. The dream was over. And all the bitter tears began.

For she learned what lay behind Eunice's growing antipathy. Her flame-haired editor had long harboured the suspicion that something was going on between Tina and Justin. And she had every right to be displeased. As she informed Tina with spitting eyes the evening she finally confronted her after hours in her office, she and Justin had been lovers for many years.

And now they were more than just lovers. 'Look at this, bitch!' she demanded, flashing a diamond engagement ring in Tina's face. 'Last night he asked me to be his wife. Justin and I are going to be married!'

'But Justin's in the States. He's away for three weeks.' Tina stood there paralysed, feeling as though she'd turned to marble. She had no feeling in any part of her body.

'I know that, you slut! He proposed over the phone! And this morning the man from Cartier's arrived on my doorstep with the ring. Justin knew I'd say yes. We've had an understanding for a long time that eventually we'd get engaged.'

A sense of nausea had swept through Tina. Suddenly, things were falling into place. So, this was why Justin had asked her to keep their romance quiet. Because he was secretly involved with Eunice.

'And now I want you out of here and off my magazine by tomorrow! You'll be paid a month's salary, but I never want to see you again!'

As Tina stared back at her, ashen-faced and dumbstruck, that mocking smile that would stick forever in Tina's memory spread maliciously over Eunice's face.

'You weren't his only trinket. He's had plenty of others before you. And, possibly, he'll have plenty more. But I don't care about that. I'm the one he's going to marry. You, my dear, were never more than his slut!'

Tina left the *Miranda* office that evening never to return—though, even if Eunice hadn't fired her, she'd have handed in her notice anyway. In the circumstances, it would have been impossible to go on working at JM Publishing.

Yet in one corner of her heart there was a tiny flicker of hope that maybe this was all just some ghastly nightmare. Justin had told her he loved her. How could Eunice's story be true?

But it was. That evening Justin phoned her from Houston. By the end of the phone call Tina's heart was in shreds.

But there was no begging, no weeping—at least, not to him, though privately she wept an ocean. Instead, she simply did what she knew she had to do. She cut him from her life. Ruthlessly. Without mercy. She would never see him or speak to him ever again.

And she hadn't—except for once, when they'd bumped into each other accidentally—until yesterday afternoon at the reception.

The phone rang, shattering Tina's reverie.

She sprang up in her seat, not even certain where she was, and blinked round in confusion at her empty office. Her heart was thundering like a steam train.

Then she sighed and relaxed, glad to be back in the present, and glanced down at her desk where her direct line was still shrilling. Shaking herself, she reached out and picked it up.

It was Mike. 'So, you're still there. Haven't you got a home to go to?' he joked. Then he continued, 'The reason I'm calling is because I've just been speaking to one of my mates—and he was telling me something I thought you ought to know...'

He was right. It was definitely something Tina ought to know.

Five minutes later, when she laid the phone down, there was a glint of steel in Tina's eyes. She reached for a piece of paper and scribbled a message, then went outside to the general office and placed it prominently on her secretary's desk for her to find first thing tomorrow morning.

'Cancel all this morning's appointments,' it said. 'Something unexpected's come up.'

Then she gathered her things and left the office, her stride firm, the spark of battle in her eyes. First thing tomorrow morning she was going to JM Publishing for a no-holds-barred confrontation with Justin!

CHAPTER THREE

AT HALF-PAST eight the following morning Tina swept through the huge doors of JM Publishing, flashing her Berry's security pass at the blinking security man on the door.

'I've come to see your boss,' she announced without pausing, and proceeded to march unstoppably across the marble-tiled hallway, heading for the bank of lifts at the back.

One stood conveniently open. She stepped inside it and quickly pressed the button for the twenty-third floor. Then, fists clenched, her heart ticking like a time bomb inside her, she was being borne aloft at high speed towards Justin's penthouse office suite.

What she was doing was rash. He would be absolutely furious with her for daring to confront him on his own territory like this. But Tina didn't give a damn. She was furious, too. She wanted some answers and she wanted them now.

In the space of a heartbeat, it seemed, she had reached the twenty-third floor and the lift doors were purring open once more. Taking a deep breath, Tina stepped out into the empty corridor. Justin's office suite was right in front of her, fronted by his secretary's imposing desk which, as Tina had been praying, was mercifully vacant. His secretary, Miss

Ronin, was notoriously hard to get past. She guarded her boss's privacy like a Rottweiler in wing-framed glasses.

On firm strides Tina crossed the expanse of silent carpet that led to the panelled door behind which Justin controlled his empire. She was wearing a red flowered dress. Red for courage. This was going to require all the courage she possessed!

She raised her fist to knock, fighting back a sudden attack of nerves. Last time she had been here, she'd been sure of her welcome. A lovesick, starry-eyed, inexperienced twenty-one-year-old who'd believed the man behind this door was her personal passport to paradise. A man she could love, respect and admire forever. A man who would always love her in return.

Hah! That was a joke! He had never loved her. And now here he was, trying to screw up her life again!

Her nerves had vanished. He would soon find out how wrong he was to think he could trample all over her again! Her spine straight, her knuckles came down hard on the polished mahogany. Then, without waiting for a response, she pushed the door open and stepped impatiently into the room beyond.

'Good morning. You're early.'

He was seated at his desk at the far end of the huge room, half caught in the light from the window behind him. And he was bent over the pile of papers that were spread out in front of him, his attention clearly absorbed in what he was doing.

He hadn't even glanced up as Tina walked into the room, and quite clearly he had assumed that she was his secretary. Only that could account for the civilised greeting!

He was in for a surprise! Tina took a couple of strides towards him and came to a halt in the middle of the room, amazed at how calm and composed she was feeling. She could feel her heart beating, but it was a calm, steady beat. Her eyes fixed on the distracted figure. 'Good morning,' she replied.

He did glance up then, sharply, his brow furrowing as he looked at her. He tossed down his pen. 'What the hell are you doing here?'

'I've come to see you.'

Tina felt a momentary tremor as the iron-grey eyes tore into her like razors. She'd been right about his reaction. He was absolutely furious.

'And how did you get in?' Justin was rising to his feet to confront her. 'No one phoned up to say you were on your way.'

'I just walked in.' Tina wanted to step back as he started to stride across the carpet towards her. But she forced herself to stand firm. 'No one tried to stop me.'

'Very clever. I suppose that's why you're here so early? Because you knew my secretary wouldn't be here yet. She as sure as hell would have stopped you!'

Right first shot and Tina didn't try to deny it. 'I had to see you,' she informed him simply. Then she added in an appeasing tone as he stood there glowering down at her. 'Besides, I thought it would be better to catch you early, before the working day got under way.'

'My working day got under way a couple of hours ago!' Flames shot from his eyes. He was not appeased. 'And the reason I start early is because I don't like to be disturbed—by phone calls and faxes and unexpected visitors. Especially unexpected visitors who would be unwelcome at any time.'

Before Tina could catch her breath, he had grabbed her by the elbow and was frog-marching her unceremoniously towards the door. 'Which is why I'm afraid I must ask you to leave!'

'I'm sorry but I'm not leaving.' Tina dug her heels into the carpet, but all that happened was that she bumped along like a piece of cargo. She dug harder, resisting him with every atom of her strength. 'I'm not leaving. I need to speak to you,' she insisted a little breathlessly.

'Write me a letter about it and maybe I'll get round to answering it.' They had reached the door. He stopped in front of it. 'Now will you leave under your own steam or do you want me to throw you out?'

'No, I don't want you to throw me out.' Tina stood her ground defiantly. 'What I want you to do is listen to what I've come to say.'

'That's not on offer. You either leave voluntarily or I throw you out. So, which of these two choices is it to be?'

He was still holding on to her arm, his fingers like vices, and he was standing over her like some Titan in a Savile Row suit. And it suddenly struck

Tina that to any observer they would have presented a comically ill-matched pair of adversaries—the tall, dark-haired man whose every pore breathed virile strength, and the slender, blonde-haired girl in the red flowered dress who looked as though she didn't have a muscle to her name.

But she did have guts.

Tina tilted her chin at him. 'What's it with you that you have to keep throwing your weight around? Why can't you behave like a normal, rational person and stop trying to intimidate me all the time?'

Justin seemed surprised at this shift in tactic. He raised dark eyebrows and looked down at her curiously for a moment, an amused smile flickering round the corners of his mouth. Then he shook his head, a look of cynicism in the dark eyes. 'I would treat you the way one normal, rational person treats another if I didn't happen to know that would be a total waste of time. You're neither normal nor rational.' His smile twisted dismissively. 'On the contrary, I would say the best word to describe you is perverse.'

And what was that supposed to mean? Did he consider her perverse because she'd cut him out of her life so ruthlessly three years ago?

Tina made a contemptuous noise. 'I would say *you're* the perverse one! You're the one whose behaviour could be called into question!'

Justin paused for just a millisecond, eyes piercing into her like rapiers. 'Perhaps there have been occasions when that was the case.' There was a merciless, sharp, cutting edge to his tone now. 'But that was due to bad judgement rather than perversity.'

As he paused to hold her gaze, it was perfectly plain what he was saying. Their entire relationship, as far as he was concerned, had been nothing but a regrettable error of judgement.

Tina knew that shouldn't bother her. That was how she thought of it too. But she felt unexpectedly wounded by the callous statement and by the accompanying callous dark look in his eyes. Just for a moment, she could think of nothing to say.

As she stood there blinking, his grip round her arm tightened. He was reaching for the door-handle as he added, 'But my powers of judgement, happily, at this moment are functioning perfectly. Which is why I want you out of my office and out of this building now!'

And with that he grabbed the door-handle, clearly intending to throw her out. But at that precise moment there was an unexpected development.

The door opened, apparently of its own volition, catching Tina a sharp stab in the small of the back. As she jerked away to avoid it she collided with Justin, who was continuing to hold her firmly by the arm. And as she stood there, pressed against him, her free hand resting on his chest, Miss Ronin, Justin's formidable secretary, walked into the room.

'Good morning, Mr Marlowe. I——'

Miss Ronin stopped in mid-sentence, eyes wide behind the wing-framed spectacles. Clearly, she was having a little difficulty interpreting the scene before her.

Tina saw her hesitation and found herself reacting automatically. Staying precisely where she was, her body jammed against Justin's, she turned to Miss Ronin with an enigmatic smile. Oh, dear, her expression said quite plainly, you've caught us!

Miss Ronin got the message. She flushed and stuttered, 'E-excuse me. I'm interrupting.' Then she began to back hurriedly out of the door.

'It's OK. You're not interrupting.' Justin was taking over, releasing his grip on Tina's arm and stepping away. 'As it happens, Miss Gordon was just about to leave.'

'I see, sir.' Poor Miss Ronin clearly didn't know what to think. She continued to hover uncomfortably in the doorway, her face glowing as brightly as the lights on a Christmas tree. Then she cleared her throat. 'There's a call for you from Hong Kong. Shall I put it through or ask them to call back?'

'Put it through.' Justin was already heading back to his desk. 'And kindly show Miss Gordon out.'

But Tina wasn't having that! As the secretary went off to transfer the call, clearly expecting Tina to follow her, Tina waited by the door until Justin had picked up his phone. Then she closed the door and crossed the room to park herself in one of the chairs opposite his desk. You're not getting rid of me as easily as that! she was thinking.

He didn't glance at her once as he spoke to his caller, though it was perfectly obvious he knew she was there. Tina could tell that by the sharp, angry angle of his jaw and by the hostile vibrations shooting at her like daggers across the desk.

Then at last he laid the phone down and Tina felt herself stiffen. Would he now resume what he had been about to do a couple of minutes ago—namely throw her bodily out of his office?

He turned slowly to face her, his eyes dark and dangerous. 'So,' he said, 'what was that little charade in front of my secretary all about? Am I supposed to read into it some deep, hidden meaning, or was it just another example of your perverse nature?'

Tina met his gaze a little uncomfortably. She'd rather been hoping he wouldn't bring that up. She assured him hastily, 'Please don't read anything into it. I was desperate, and desperate situations call for desperate measures.'

'Is that so?'

Justin sat back in his chair and steepled his long, tanned fingers beneath his chin. Eyes searching, he looked across at her. Then, unexpectedly, he smiled.

'Mind you, I'm not complaining. It was really rather enjoyable. I'd forgotten how well your body fits against mine, and how warm and soft and welcoming it feels.'

Tina blushed to her hair roots. She'd been struggling to deny it, but the same thoughts, if only for an instant, had also occurred to her.

It had felt quite breathtakingly familiar and not at all unpleasant to be standing there so intimately with him, the warmth of his hard, masculine body flowing through her. And her hand against his chest had felt almost as though she was caressing him, just as she might have done once, long ago.

But she'd only felt that for an instant and it was definitely not why she'd done it.

Smothering her blushes, Tina pointed out to him. 'Your secretary certainly seemed to think you were enjoying it.'

That was why she'd done it. To compromise him in the eyes of his secretary. It had been an automatic thing. She'd seen her chance and grabbed it.

She eyed him. 'I would say that puts you in a difficult position. I mean, you can't very well throw me out now. It would look as though you were trying to cover up your tracks.' She smiled as another wicked thought occurred to her. 'Especially if I were to make a bit of a scene.'

'And no doubt you would do that?'

'If you pushed me to it.'

'If I pushed you?' Justin smiled a frankly cynical smile. 'I suspect it probably wouldn't take much pushing. As I recall, you have a taste for scenes.'

Tina felt the colour momentarily drain from her face. She knew what he was referring to: their last meeting three years ago, when they had bumped into each other accidentally outside Charing Cross Station and she had flung at him all the bitter bile in her heart.

But for him to accuse her of having enjoyed that was callous and unfeeling. Surely he knew she had been out of her head with grief?

Inwardly she shivered and stared down at the carpet, its rich woven colours blurring before her eyes. That had been the worst time of her life. She had barely survived it. And there had been moments when she had seriously doubted that she would.

But she had. And now it was all behind her. Though he might try, he couldn't touch her with his cruel references to the past.

Tina raised her eyes to his again, her vision once more sharp and clear. 'And you don't like them, do you? Scenes, I mean,' she elaborated. She twisted her lips into what she hoped was a sneer edged with just a touch of cruel amusement. 'I wonder if you'll have a scene on your hands when your fiancée gets to hear about what your secretary saw when she walked through the door a moment ago.'

'And what did my secretary see?'

'Well, nothing, in reality. But clearly she thought she was seeing something.' Tina levelled him a look of mock-concern. 'And such misunderstandings can lead to trouble.'

Let's hope, she added to herself with happy malice. That little bonus had not been in her mind at the time, but now it definitely rather appealed to her.

Justin met her gaze steadily and said nothing for a moment. With one elegant tanned hand he reached out casually and lifted a silver paperknife from where it lay on his desk. Was he about to aim it at her? Tina wondered a little dubiously. He certainly looked as though he would very much like to.

But he did not. Weighing it lightly in his hand, he simply smiled. 'Miss Ronin, I can assure you, is most discreet.'

'Ah. That's a relief.' Tina's tone was heavy with irony. 'After all,' she added, 'your fiancée is a woman with even more of a taste for scenes than me.' Anyone who'd ever worked for JM Publishing knew that!

Tina regarded him curiously. 'How do you put up with it?' Then she shrugged. 'I suppose you're used to it by now.'

'I suppose I am.'

He smiled back at her uncaringly and twirled the silver paperknife like a baton between his fingers. And Tina found herself acknowledging that she was probably miles from the truth. During their time together the volatile Eunice had undoubtedly learned to control her temper, at least with Justin. He would never put up with her angry eruptions.

Unless, of course, Tina amended, love had made him more tolerant. Maybe he loved Eunice so much he simply put up with her tantrums.

At that thought, illogically, she felt a cold twist inside her, as though someone had reached out and touched her heart with ice.

She pushed the feeling from her. What was she thinking of? He could love the dreadful woman to distraction for all she cared!

As though to prove that to herself, she deliberately pursued the subject. She leaned back in her chair, her demeanour studiedly casual.

'I hear wedding-bells are in the air. Congratulations. I'm sure you'll be very happy. You're perfectly suited.'

Justin couldn't have cared less about her feelings on the subject. His dark eyes looked through her as he twirled the paperknife arrogantly. 'Am I to understand that's why you're here? To offer your congratulations on my forthcoming wedding?' He smiled a scathing smile. 'Most touching, but quite unnecessary. A simple greetings card would have been sufficient.'

Sarcastic pig! Tina glared at him. 'No, that's not why I'm here.' So, it was true, she was thinking. This long-delayed marriage was finally going ahead. Well, that was fine. Good luck to them, she told herself.

She reached into her bag and drew out his handkerchief—which she had carefully laundered to remove that unsettling scent!—and tossed it towards him across the desk.

'I've come to give you this...and, more importantly——'

But as she was about to elaborate on her real reason for being there, Justin rudely cut in, 'You still haven't told me how you managed to get in the building.' He held the silver paperknife still for a moment. He hadn't even acknowledged the return of his handkerchief. 'How did you get past the security man at the door?'

'I showed him my Berry's pass.' Tina couldn't suppress a smile. She'd been rather impressed by her own bravado.

'Your Berry's pass? And he let you in on the strength of that?' Justin's tone suggested he didn't share her enjoyment of the joke.

'I only flashed it at him very quickly and said I was going to see his boss. He didn't have time to see it properly.'

'It's his job to see it properly.' There was a tightness round his jaw. 'I can see you're feeling very pleased with your little trick, but I'm afraid you've just lost that man his job.' His gaze darkened. 'Not that I expect you to lose any sleep over that.'

'You're kidding!' Tina was appalled. She sat forward in her seat. 'You wouldn't really fire that poor man because of what I did?'

'Not because of what you did, but because of what he failed to do. He's there to make sure only people with passes get through the door.'

'But it wasn't his fault!' Justin really was serious! He really intended to fire that poor security man! Tina searched frantically in her brain for an excuse to take the blame off him. 'He probably recognised me and that was why he let me in. After all, I used to work here.'

'I hadn't forgotten.' Justin's tone was cutting. 'You worked here briefly, just to gather some experience, before moving on to better things.'

How well he remembered. That was what she'd said to him at Charing Cross Station, hurling all her hurt and anger and despair at him in a helpless torrent of abuse. Though she'd meant none of it, of course. It had all been a lie. A lie she had invented just to hurt him. Just to pay back a fraction of how much he'd hurt her.

Tina glanced down into her lap as the memories briefly overwhelmed her. Then she looked up at him again. 'Don't take it out on that security man. He doesn't deserve it. I didn't give him a chance to stop me.'

Justin's dark eyes looked right through her. 'Spare me the tears,' he told her, as though he'd seen her sudden emotion and mistaken it for feigned sympathy for the security man. 'I know all about that famous altruism of yours. Just get on and tell me why you're here.'

'First tell me you won't sack that man.' Tina ignored the insult. 'It was my fault. I take full responsibility.'

'I'll let you know.' Justin regarded her coldly. Then he glanced at his watch. 'And now, if you don't mind, either tell me what you're doing here or else kindly leave.'

There was no point in insisting. It would get her nowhere. Tina made a mental note to check at a later date whether he had sacked the security man or not. Then she leaned forward in her seat and finally revealed what had brought her here.

'It's about *Scope*.' What else would bring her to his office? 'Yesterday I tried to persuade you to tell me what your plans were——'

'And I told you you'd find out in good time.' His tone was impatient. 'I don't like having to repeat myself.' The paperknife in his hand flashed a warning as he twirled it. 'So, if you've just come here to go over all that again, I suggest you leave now.'

'I haven't come just to go over all that again. There's been a development. It seems that someone already knows your plans.'

'And who might that be?'

Tina glared at him. 'Your fiancée.'

How come, she wondered fleetingly, she never quite managed to say Eunice's name? But she hurried swiftly on, ignoring that question.

'She's been spreading stories among certain freelances who do work for us—writers and photographers and models and the like—that it's a waste of time doing any work for *Scope* these days. She's been saying that *Scope*'s days are definitely numbered, that as soon as the take-over's gone through we're to be folded into *Miranda*.'

She thinned her lips at him. 'I don't like these methods. If something's going to happen, there should be an official announcement.'

Justin's expression had altered. He became very still as he looked back at her. Tina had the feeling that for the first time she had his full attention.

Eyes like pebbles, he demanded, 'Where did you get this information?'

'I got it from Mike. Mike Laing of Arts Studios. Your fiancée apparently had a word with one of his friends. And I have reason to believe she's also had a word with one of our writers.'

For this explained, Tina had decided, the reason why one of her star freelance writers had handed in such a sloppy, unprofessional job. The Red

Dragon had advised her she was wasting her time writing for *Scope*.

'Mike Laing.' As Justin repeated the name, his eyes flitted over Tina's face. 'Yes,' he observed, 'I suppose Mike would tell you anything he'd heard.'

Tina felt a prickle of curiosity at the oddness of that remark. There'd been an inflexion in his tone that seemed to suggest something.

Then in a flash she understood. Justin was under the impression that there was something going on between herself and Mike!

Was this yet another rumour that was going around? she wondered. And in her surprise at the very possibility she felt herself blush. She saw Justin notice the blush and reach a conclusion. Now he *definitely* believed there was a romance going on!

Tina was on the point of denying it, but she bit her tongue in time. It was none of Justin's business. None of her private life was. And besides, she found it really rather pleasing that he should believe she was romantically involved with someone else.

She frowned at him and demanded the answer she had come for. 'So? Are these stories your fiancée's been spreading true?'

He did not answer immediately. He sat back in his leather swivel chair and regarded her thoughtfully for a moment. Then his expression changed. One eyebrow lifted. 'Why, what do you plan to do if they are?'

'Fight you.'

'Fight me?' He smiled. 'But you can't win. I'm your boss, remember—or will be soon. To beat you all I have to do is fire you.'

'But you won't fire me. At least, not immediately.'

'And what makes you think that?'

'Because you want your pound of flesh.'

Tina sat back, narrowing her eyes at him and recalling the threats he'd made. She'd thought about them a lot, though she'd tried not to let them worry her. After all, the worst he could to her was fire her, and though she would hate to lose her job she would find another one. Besides, as she told him again now, 'You wouldn't fire me right away. Let's face it, that wouldn't be any fun.'

As soon as she'd said it, she rather regretted the way she'd worded that. And, sure enough, Justin picked it up.

'So, you think I'm looking for fun with you?' he responded with a wicked smile. He twirled the paperknife. 'That sounds like an acceptable bonus.'

'Not *with* me. At my expense.' Tina said it firmly, though, in spite of herself, she had definitely felt a quick flicker of excitement. Sex with Justin had indeed been a lot of fun.

She banished that thought instantly, wondering where on earth it had sprung from, and told him again, 'You won't fire me immediately. I reckon I'll be around long enough to put up a good fight.'

She held his gaze steadily. What mattered was *Scope*. She must find a way to save her beloved magazine.

But then he surprised her. 'So, you're going to fight me, are you? Funny, I thought negotiations would be more your style.'

Tina felt slightly thrown. 'Does that mean negotiations are possible?'

Frankly, she would prefer that option to a fight— she had scant hope of winning an out-and-out fight with Justin!—but she hadn't expected that anything so civilised would be on the agenda.

She sat up in her seat. 'Of course I'm prepared to negotiate. I'm prepared to negotiate all you like.' She wasn't quite sure what there was to negotiate, but at least he was open to discussion.

Justin smiled—not quite a tiger's smile, though it definitely had an edge to it. Then he asked her, seeming to pluck the question at random from the air, 'Does anyone else from *Scope* know you're here?'

'No one knows I'm here. I haven't had a chance to tell them yet.'

'But you plan to, of course?'

'Naturally. Of course I do.'

Foolishly, she blushed. There was something odd about the way he was looking at her. And, as he noted her blush, his eyes seemed to narrow. He tossed down the paperknife and glanced at his watch. 'It's getting late. I'm afraid I'm going to have to ask you to leave now.'

'What?' Tina blinked at him. 'Aren't we going to discuss it now?'

'No, I'm afraid not.' Justin was rising to his feet. 'You've already taken up more than enough of my time.'

Tina was uncertain what to do next. If she insisted, she might blow things. And she didn't want to do that. They seemed to have made some kind of progress.

'When, then?' she demanded, reluctantly standing up too.

'Soon.' He was sweeping past her and leading her towards the door. And his demeanour had altered. There was a sudden cold detachment. Probably just some business worry that's suddenly struck him, Tina told herself, though, illogically, she had the feeling that the cause of the change in him was her.

He had reached the door and was pulling it open. 'I'll be in touch with you,' he said.

'I'll be waiting.' Tina glanced up at him as he stood aside to let her past. 'I'd like to start negotiating as soon as possible.'

'Don't worry, we shall.'

He barely returned her glance, but as Tina headed past the imposing desk of Miss Ronin, who, ever the soul of discretion, didn't even glance up, she could tell he was still standing in the doorway watching her. He was still watching her as she pressed the button to summon the lift.

The lift arrived and the lift doors opened. Tina stepped inside and pressed the button for the ground floor. Then, as she turned around to face Justin again, he spoke.

'Don't worry we shall have our negotiations,' he said softly. The smile on his lips was as cold as winter. And twice as deadly as he added in a tone of pure malice, 'And I, as you so rightly predicted, shall have my pound of flesh.'

In that instant Tina knew she had fallen into some trap. She felt a flare of panic. What did he mean by that? She'd thought the worst he could do to her was throw her out of her job, but now all at once she wasn't sure.

But she only had time to mouth a silent protest as the lift doors closed and she was borne silently away.

CHAPTER FOUR

TINA left JM Publishing and took a taxi back to Berry's in a state of almost total confusion.

What was Justin up to? What kind of trap had she just walked into? What exactly did he have in mind when he spoke about having his pound of flesh?

Or was he simply tormenting her, just for the hell of it? That was perfectly possible. Perhaps there was really no trap at all.

She crossed her fingers and prayed that was the case. That soon he'd ring her and invite her back to negotiate—though what sort of negotiations he had in mind she really couldn't imagine. So, just wait and see—and try to think positive! she told herself.

Tina told no one about her visit to JM Publishing, in spite of having said to Justin that she would. It was all too complicated and confusing and unpleasant. And there was too much personal animosity mixed in. Besides, for the moment, there was really nothing to tell. She would confide in the others when something concrete had been achieved.

Back at the *Scope* office, Tina immersed herself in work and, mercifully, the day passed quickly enough—though the minute she stepped out of the office to go home all the questions started milling around in her brain again.

Would Justin really ring her? What should she do if he didn't? Was there some trap? What was he plotting for her?

What's wrong with you? she chastised herself. You're acting crazy. And that bothered her. Normally, she didn't act crazy. Normally, she dealt with things in a calm and rational manner. But for some reason all her calmness and rationality seemed to have departed.

Was it Justin doing this to her? The thought appalled her. He was the last person she should allow to get to her in this manner. After all, what was Justin to her? Just a heap of bad memories. Memories she had long ago consigned to her mental rubbish bin.

With a snap of will-power she pulled herself together. She would not let him mess up her present. She would simply deal with the problems he had brought as she dealt with any other problems. And, to prove that, tonight she wouldn't give him another thought.

Back home Tina deliberately kept herself busy, writing letters and making phone calls—and fixing up an interview for Saturday morning with a couple in the Cotswolds she needed to speak to if she was ever going to pull that troublesome article together. At least that was one problem she seemed to have under control!

Finally, just after midnight, she fell into bed.

And that was when her brain played a cruel trick on her. For as she drifted off to sleep all the memories she'd tried to banish came, like some black crow settling on her pillow, to confront her in her dreams.

'Justin and I are going to be married. You, my dear, were never more than his slut!'

It was three years ago and she was back in her old flat, pacing the floor in a turmoil of agony the evening after her horrific meeting with Eunice.

And she couldn't believe what Eunice had told her. Surely, it was impossible? she kept telling herself over and over. Justin loved her. He had said so, often. Eunice must be lying, playing some bizarre, sadistic trick on her. If she could just get hold of Justin and speak to him, he would tell her it had all been a hoax.

It was just after ten-thirty when the phone in the hall rang. Tina snatched it up with rigid fingers and held it, heart thumping, to her ear. And from the beep on the line she knew instantly it was long-distance.

'Hello?' she said, her mouth as dry as dust.

'Tina, how are you?'

He sounded normal, not the least bit like a man hiding some terrible secret.

Encouraged, Tina struggled to sound normal too. 'I'm fine,' she lied, her hand like a claw round the receiver. 'How about you? How are things going over there?'

'They're going great. I'm frantically busy. It's non-stop work. I hardly have time to eat or sleep.'

Justin laughed with wry humour as he added, 'The Americans certainly know how to put in a day's work.'

Every word he spoke was making Tina more hopeful. He sounded just like always, warm and humorous. As she listened to him, Tina felt herself relax a little. What Eunice had told her couldn't possibly be true.

And for a moment she was tempted not even to broach the subject. If it was all just some silly lie, after all, what was the point?

But she knew that was the fear deep inside her speaking. She had to speak up. She had to know the truth.

Taking a deep breath, she plunged in. 'Justin...I was speaking to Eunice today...'

There was the minutest of pauses, but definitely a pause. 'Oh, yes?' he said. There was a guarded note in his voice.

Tina could feel the room suddenly swimming around her. A sick feeling rose from the pit of her stomach to lodge, as heavy as a stone, in her throat.

She licked her dry lips. 'She told me,' she said.

This time the pause was much longer and more ominous. Then Justin said with a sigh, 'Oh, dear. She told you, did she?'

'Yes, she did.'

Tina swallowed drily. She could no longer focus; she felt numb from head to toe and she had the giddy sensation that suddenly she was tumbling into some bottomless black pit.

Through bloodless lips she demanded, 'Justin, is it true?'

Again he sighed. 'Look, I'm really sorry. I didn't want Eunice to be the one to tell you. I was going to tell you myself tonight.'

The room had turned black. Tina could barely stand upright. It was though someone had sucked all of her insides out of her.

'I see,' she only just managed to answer. 'You were going to tell me tonight.'

'Look, don't get upset. I'll explain everything when I see you. I'm sorry you had to hear it from Eunice.'

'I'm sorry too.'

She was standing there in agony. How could he be so offhand and casual about it? How could he say something as cruelly trivial as 'don't get upset'?

'But it doesn't really matter who I heard it from, does it? What matters is that you lied to me and misled me.'

There was anger in Tina's voice now as she stood there fighting for breath, aware that a helpless storm of grief and fury was gathering, like a heavy dark cloud, inside her. She could feel it pressing against her ribs, rising up to choke her throat, threatening to explode like a tornado at any moment.

And there was really no point in continuing this conversation. Every word he spoke was like a dagger through her heart and she could no longer trust herself to remain coherent. Any minute now her control would desert her and she would break down into a flood of hysterical weeping. And she had far too much pride to degrade herself like that. Especially when it was so clear that he didn't give a damn.

She choked back the tears. 'How could you?' she accused him. 'You're nothing but a rotten, two-faced bastard!' Then, before the tears could start, she banged down the phone.

Tina was still standing there in a state of frozen misery, struggling to absorb the horror of what had just happened and how her whole life had suddenly been turned on its head, when the phone began to ring again.

It was Justin, of course. She knew that instinctively. He had called back to soothe her, to offer excuses and silken lies. But Tina was damned if she would hear them.

She snapped the wall plug from its socket, stopping the ringing instantly, vowing that to-morrow she would have her number changed. Then she stared in rigid silence at the silent phone for a moment, trying not to acknowledge how deeply terrifying that silence was.

For there was a terrible cold finality to it. That silence was telling her that her love-affair with Justin had just ended.

The tears were rising up inside her, threatening to choke her, and there was a pain inside her so fierce that she could scarcely breathe. She struggled to fight it, but it was a pain beyond fighting. She threw back her head and let out a helpless cry of anguish.

'Why? When I loved you? How could you do it? Don't you know I would have given my very life for you?'

And suddenly she was sobbing, helplessly, uncontrollably, sinking to the floor as though to drown in her tears, her hands covering her face, her whole body trembling, weeping her heart out with a sorrow that would never end.

And that was when, with a violent start, she awoke.

Tina sat up in bed, catching her breath, and stared into the darkness of her bedroom for a moment. Her whole body was trembling. Her heart was clattering inside her. She could feel the cool dampness of tears on her face.

Shakily, she reached out and switched on the bedside lamp, and felt her breathing instantly grow easier as light flooded the room, shattering the lurking shadow of the dream. Then she slipped from the bed, giving herself a small shake. What she needed was a glass of warm milk to calm her down.

She pulled on her dressing-gown and went through to the kitchen, took some milk from the fridge and poured it into a pan. But, as she switched on the gas, though she was feeling much more calm now, her mind was still fixed on the events of three years ago and, specifically, on what had happened after that phone call.

The weeks that had followed had been unbearable. Tina had heard through the grapevine that a couple of days after she'd spoken to Justin Eunice had gone flying off to the States. Only Tina knew why, for the engagement hadn't been made public, and the thought of Justin and Eunice together had simply made her agony worse.

Not that it should matter to me, she'd told herself bitterly. After all, when it comes down it, nothing has really changed. He's been seeing Eunice all along, right from the beginning. The only difference is that, before, I didn't know it.

How clever he'd been at keeping all the bits of his life secret! No one had even known he had *one* woman, let alone a pair of them! Or several of them, if Eunice was to be believed! And why shouldn't Eunice be believed? Tina had decided. It seemed Eunice was the only one who really knew the man behind the mask.

It wasn't until nearly six weeks later that Justin had finally returned to London.

His intended three-week stint, Tina had always supposed, had been extended to accommodate a celebratory holiday with his new fiancée. But Tina hadn't cared. It had given her time to recover. By the time he got back she'd moved to a new flat and started a new job as a sub-editor-writer on *Scope*. She was doing her very best to put the past behind her.

And she'd prayed that she and Justin might never meet again. Though, of course, she reflected now, as she poured the warm milk into a mug and seated herself at the kitchen table, that prayer was destined not to be answered. She was to bump into him just a couple of weeks after his return, quite accidentally, outside Charing Cross Station.

She was going in and he was coming out, and Tina didn't even see him till she almost walked right into him when he deliberately stepped in front of her.

'And where are you off to in such a hurry? On some urgent errand for your new magazine, perhaps?'

At the sound of his deep voice, Tina felt her blood freeze. She looked up at him, the colour draining from her face.

'Yes,' she said, feeling her heart knock against her ribs.

It was two months since she'd seen him, but it could have been yesterday. She felt a rush of emotion, familiar and vivid, mingle with the pain that lived in her heart these days. Just for a moment, illogically, it felt wonderful to see him. She felt like smiling and reaching out to touch him.

But the feeling was crushed instantly. There was no smile in Justin's eyes. Instead, as they looked down at her, they were as cold and hard as stones.

'I've been hearing about your new job.' His tone was stony too. 'I suppose I ought to congratulate you,' he said.

It was like looking at a stranger, Tina found herself thinking. Last time they'd been together, he'd been kissing her and caressing her and telling her how he could never love anyone else. And she, meaning every word of it, had been telling him the same.

She felt a rush of grief inside her. How he had betrayed her! And suddenly she longed to beat him with her fists, to let all the pain pour out of her and demand to know why.

But she stifled her emotions and answered his question. 'Yes, I've got a new job. And I'm enjoying it very much.'

It was three weeks now since she'd joined the staff of *Scope*, a brand-new magazine whose very first issue was due to hit the bookstands in one week's time. At least in that area of her life she'd had a lucky break. After her departure from *Miranda*, she'd immediately found a new job.

'You're writing features, I hear?'

'Yes, I'm doing a lot of writing.'

'So, it would seem your experience on *Miranda* did you good.'

It was not so much a question as an accusation. And at the openly hostile expression on his face Tina found herself wondering what lay at the back of his strange attitude. She, surely, was the one with good reason to be hostile? Did he have any idea of the agony he had caused her? His hostility made no sense. No sense whatsoever. He had absolutely nothing to be hostile about!

But he was glaring at her with the hatchet eyes of a man who obviously believed he had.

Tina answered his question. 'Yes, I learned a lot on *Miranda*.' And suddenly, before the words were properly out, she realised why he was angry. He resented the fact that she'd quit JM Publishing and, armed with what she'd learnt there, gone to work for another company. Whatever Eunice had told him about the reason why she'd left, she obviously hadn't told him the whole truth. For it was clear he had no idea that Eunice had fired her. He'd expected her still to be there, waiting meekly at her desk, when he arrived back from the States with his new fiancée on his arm!

Her heart cracked. It was outrageous! How could he be so unfeeling? For he must know that she now knew about his engagement—since she'd got back Eunice had been flashing her diamond ring all around London. Yet he'd expected her to stay on like some blindly faithful puppy. And what else had he expected? she wondered angrily.

He was saying to her in that cutting tone, 'I'm so glad we were able to be of use to you. All the time we spent on training you wasn't wasted after all.'

As he spoke, he let his eyes travel over her contemptuously, yet with an intimacy so acute it was almost physical. It was the kind of look a man might give to a whore.

And that was when Tina understood something else. Not only had he expected her to stay on in his employ, he had also expected her to stay on as his lover. His vanity was so huge that he had taken it for granted that she would agree to continue as before.

She was to be his secret lover, there on hand for him to enjoy, whenever he happened to feel so disposed.

Tina felt sick at the thought. That was adding insult to injury. As the anger whipped through her, crackling like lightning, the last vestiges of any longing to bare her pain to him vanished. Suddenly, all that filled her was the need to strike back.

That simmering anger proved inspirational. In the blink of an eye she'd figured out what would hurt him most.

Tina straightened and looked at him, suddenly feeling as heartless as he was. 'I don't deny that my time with your company was useful.' She twisted a smile at him and fixed him with a cold look. 'That's why I joined your company in the first place—because I knew how useful it would be.' She raised disdainful eyebrows. 'But I never intended staying. My time at JM Publishing was just a springboard, a first step on the way to better things. As soon as I'd learned all I could, I always planned on moving on.

'Forgive me.' She smiled a smile as cold as winter. 'I hope you weren't expecting loyalty or anything so old-fashioned?' Then she paused and shrugged before delivering her final blow, the one that would really put him in his place.

'And I hope our little liaison didn't confuse you. Though, you being a man of the world, I'm sure you understood. All you were to me was a means to an end. It sounds a little heartless, but I was only out for what I could get, and getting close to you simply made things easier to get. It's always a good idea to be well in with one's boss.'

She had reached him. She had definitely reached him, Tina realised with a dart of triumph as something at the back of his eyes retreated. Quite clearly, that was the last thing he'd been expecting to hear.

'No need to explain.' Instantly, he had recovered and that look at the back of his eyes had vanished. The dark gaze bored into her. 'It doesn't merit an explanation.' Then he smiled and added, cutting her heart to ribbons. 'Anyway, I'm not complaining. It was fun while it lasted. You're definitely one of the tastiest little bits of crumpet I've ever had.'

Then, with another little smile, he was turning away dismissively and sweeping past her out of the station.

That was the last time they had spoken, until that day at the reception when Tina had walked into him and spilt champagne all over herself. For, though they'd seen each other from time to time at various press functions over the years, each had always scrupulously ignored the other. What, after all, was there to say?

Tina drained her mug of milk and laid it on the kitchen table with a sigh. There had been times when she'd regretted those lies she'd told him that had turned him so implacably against her. Though that was not why she regretted them. She didn't care that he hated her. It was simply that lies were not Tina's way, and she feared sometimes that she'd rather blackened her soul with such a huge one.

For it had been huge. A million miles from the truth. Not even a tiny bit had she ever used Justin.

For her sins, and with all her heart, all she had ever done was love him.

Tina stood up and crossed to the sink to rinse out her cup. She was feeling perfectly calm again, all her past nightmares behind her. She yawned. It was time to go back to sleep.

But as she headed back to the bedroom and climbed beneath the sheets it struck her that perhaps she had another reason now to regret those lies she'd told Justin three years ago. Those lies had made him hate her and now he was out for revenge. He was out to get his pound of flesh.

Well, let him try. He didn't scare her. Tina clenched her fists beneath the sheets. And if it did come to a fight, then she would fight him, tooth and nail. With every weapon she could lay her hands on.

A mental image rose up of the two of them locked in mortal combat. And, as she drifted off to sleep, she had a smile on her face.

Tina decided over breakfast the following morning that if Justin's promised phone call didn't materialise by lunchtime she'd be forced to take matters into her own hands and ring him. She wasn't going to sit around and wait forever. The matter was urgent. They needed to talk soon. And, besides, this was Friday. She'd like something fixed up before the weekend.

But just before eleven the phone on her desk rang. She picked it up and was astonished to find herself speaking to Justin's secretary, Miss Ronin.

Miss Ronin was brief. 'Mr Marlowe would like to see you at his office at three o'clock this afternoon. Will that be convenient, Miss Gordon?'

Tina answered without bothering to consult her diary. 'Yes, that'll be convenient. I'll be there.' Then she laid down the phone and sat back, satisfied, in her chair. Nothing would stop her from keeping that appointment!

But just after one, as she was about to nip out for a quick lunch, a message came through on the fax machine. It was from Maggie, her editor, dictated from her sick-bed in hospital. 'Stand by for a phone call at two-thirty,' it said.

Damn! Tina cursed. This was most inconvenient. But she had to take Maggie's call. It could be something important.

She forgot her lunch and immediately phoned Miss Ronin. 'Can we possibly put the meeting back half an hour?' she requested. 'Something unexpected's come up.'

The reply was instant and negative. 'I'm afraid not, Miss Gordon. Mr Marlowe said three o'clock or nothing.'

'Is he there? Can I have a word with him?'

'No, I'm afraid he's not here.' Miss Ronin paused. 'Do you wish me to cancel?'

'No, definitely not.' Tina didn't hesitate. 'I'll be there,' she told Miss Ronin. *Somehow*, she promised herself.

She ordered a taxi to wait downstairs from two-thirty—a bit of an extravagance, but this was an emergency! If Maggie's call was on time and didn't take more than a few minutes she still had plenty of time to make it by three. And who knew—she crossed her fingers—Maggie might even phone early!

At two-twenty she was sitting poised by her phone, already wearing her jacket, her bag on the desk in front of her, ready to make a dash the minute the call was over. At two-twenty-five she was picking her fingers nervously and glanced at her watch every five seconds. At two-thirty she was very nearly crawling up the wall.

The call came through at two thirty-two precisely, and, really, Tina thought impatiently, it was a total waste of time. Maggie was simply phoning to check that everything was OK as regards the day-to-day running of the magazine.

'Everything's fine,' Tina assured her. 'Don't worry about a thing. Just you concentrate on getting better.'

As she laid down the phone she glanced in dismay at her watch. It was two thirty-six. Could she still make it in time?

Seconds later, she was hurtling down the stairs to the waiting taxi, throwing herself into the back seat and demanding, 'Hurry! Please!'

The driver did his best, but the traffic was daunting. It seemed that every corner they turned there was another traffic jam.

But all the same, miraculously, it was only two minutes past three when they drew up outside the JM building. Tina sighed with relief. She was hardly late at all! Everything was going to be fine.

She had barely stepped from the taxi when she realised how wrong she was.

A tall, dark figure was striding across the pavement, heading for the sleek black executive Bentley that was waiting at the side of the road. Tina felt her heart stop. Surely not! It was Justin! He hadn't waited for her after all!

The next instant she was flying across the pavement towards him. 'I'm here!' she called out. 'Hang on a minute!'

The chauffeur in the front seat had already switched on the engine, and Justin was standing with his hand on the rear door-handle, getting ready to climb into the Bentley.

He turned briefly to look at her as she came staggering towards him. 'You're late,' he said. 'The meeting's off.'

'But it can't be! I'm only two minutes late! There was a phone call. I couldn't help it. And the traffic was awful.'

'That's not my problem.' Justin was unbending. 'Like I said, the meeting's off. I have another appointment.'

'But you can't! Please don't go! This is important!' As he was about to climb inside, Tina grabbed his arm to restrain him. 'We have to talk! This is important. You promised!'

'You surprise me.' With a cold smile Justin had turned to face her, as she stood there, still desperately holding on to his arm. 'Where your own interests are involved you're usually more careful. But you blew it this time. There'll be no negotiations today. In fact, quite possibly, there'll be no negotiations at all.'

'You wouldn't! You promised! Please don't say that! I'm sorry I'm late. I couldn't help it.'

But her pleading was pointless. He'd already snatched his arm free, shaking her off the way a dog shook off a flea. Then he was climbing into the vast dark interior of the Bentley.

'How can you do this? It isn't fair! You promised!'

Tina's usual poise had suddenly slipped away from her, as she stood there in a state of total helplessness, watching as he reached out to pull the door shut.

Damn him! she was thinking. Look what I'm reduced to! Virtually prostrating myself in a public street before the man I loathe most in the world!

But then, at the very last minute, he relented.

'OK, I'll give you one more chance. Come to my house in Gloucestershire tomorrow afternoon.' He reached into his inside pocket, pulled out a card and handed it to her with a narrow, mocking smile. 'You're going to be in the area anyway, so it'll be no problem for you to drop by.'

Then he slammed the door shut and signalled to the chauffeur to drive on.

Tina stared down at the card in her hand in a state of total perplexity as the black Bentley disappeared into the busy Mayfair traffic. How did he know she was going to Gloucestershire tomorrow? Damn the man! Had he been spying on her again?

And why, she wondered, raising her eyes to glare after him, did he want her to visit him at his home? Knowing Justin, there had to be some highly dubious reason.

She felt a shiver go through her. Was this all part of his trap?

CHAPTER FIVE

MAYBE I won't go. Why should I run whenever he crooks his finger? Besides, I just know he's up to no good.

Tina was sitting in one of the window-seats that overlooked the pretty gardens of the little Cotswolds pub where she had stopped off for lunch. And though she had just completed an excellent morning's work—the interview she'd come to do was safely on the tape recorder in her bag—she was feeling far from relaxed and happy. What was she going to do about that invitation of Justin's?

Also in her bag was the card Justin had handed her yesterday, printed with the address of his Gloucestershire home—which, incidentally, she hadn't even known he possessed. And, though she'd looked it up on her map and seen that it was only a few miles away, she was still undecided about whether she should go.

Sure, she wanted to speak to him, but going to his house might be unwise. A bit like dropping in on a funnel-web spider.

Tina took a mouthful of cool lager and sighed a troubled sigh. Maybe she ought to wait till Monday and call on him at his office. She couldn't quite define why, but she'd feel less threatened there.

'Here you are, Miss. Here's your ploughman's special.'

Tina broke off from her troubled thoughts as the smiling barman, negotiating his way between the crowded, noisy tables, arrived to lay her lunch before her.

'Thanks. It looks delicious.' She glanced down with approval at the mouth-watering-looking assortment of cheeses and cooked meats. 'This is precisely what I need,' she told him.

He threw her a wink. 'Enjoy,' he told her.

Tina did just that, for it was quite as delicious as it looked and she hadn't realised till she started eating just how hungry she was. She'd made an early start this morning, leaving just before nine to make it in time for her appointment at ten-thirty. She'd known she'd have to take it slow along the motorway. Her temperamental old Panda wasn't up to high speeds! So it was rather a long time since she'd last eaten.

She took another mouthful of her lager and glanced around her, feeling herself begin to relax a bit. She would decide after she'd eaten whether or not to drop in on Justin. Though more and more she suspected she probably wouldn't.

Maybe she'd just go for a drive instead and look for a bed and breakfast for tonight. For she'd decided that, since she was here, she'd make a weekend of it. It was such a picturesque area. And the break would do her good.

Smiling, she sighed and turned to glance out of the window at the garden dappled with soft

September sunshine. No, she resolved, she definitely wouldn't drop in on Justin. Why should she ruin a perfectly pleasant day?

But in that same instant the day ceased to be pleasant. Tina froze in her seat, very nearly dropping her knife and fork, as a gleaming white Mercedes pulled into the car park, then the two people inside proceeded to climb out.

It can't be, Tina thought dully. I couldn't be this unlucky. This is stretching the fatal arm of coincidence too far!

The two people from the Mercedes were heading towards the pub now—a tall, dark-haired man in a leather jacket and navy trousers and a wafer-thin redhead, dressed from head to toe in Versace.

It couldn't be, but it was. It was Justin and Eunice.

Tina stared paralysed for a moment, scarcely able to believe it. It couldn't be coincidence. He must have known she was here. She felt a sudden rush of anger and alarm inside her. He really was keeping tabs on her! What evil was he plotting?

But maybe she'd been wrong, she decided hopefully a moment later as the two of them, without even a glance in her direction, seated themselves in one of the more private banquettes in the far corner. It would appear that, after all, their showing up here was a coincidence. And, thankfully, they hadn't seen her. They were totally unaware of her presence.

When Justin got up to go to the bar to order some drinks, Tina was sorely tempted to dive beneath the table. But such measures quite clearly were unnecessary, she decided as she studied the closed, preoccupied expression on his face. He seemed lost in his own thoughts, totally unaware of his surroundings. Maybe it's love, Tina thought bitchily. No one exists for him but Eunice.

She tried not to keep peering at him as he took his drinks and left the bar, and made an effort to eat some more of her ploughman's special. But her appetite had gone and it was more than she could manage to stop glancing every few seconds at the banquette in the corner where an animated and intense conversation was going on.

I'll bet, Tina found herself thinking, they're discussing the arrangements for the wedding. Well, good luck to them. But she hated the way her stomach squeezed at the thought.

And then, about fifteen minutes later, there was an unexpected development.

Tina glanced up to see both Justin and Eunice on their feet and heading together for the door. A moment later, craning her neck, she saw them embracing outside, exchanging an intimate, long-drawn-out kiss, and then Eunice was climbing into a taxi and, still with that rapt look on his face, Justin was waving her off.

Whatever the reason for this separate departure, it looked as though Tina's ordeal was over. She continued to watch Justin, feeling the tension in her slacken, fully expecting him to head for the white Mercedes.

But he didn't. Instead, he turned straight back into the pub. A moment later, to her dismay, he was striding towards her.

Tina turned to marble as he seated himself opposite her. 'Well, now,' he was saying. 'Aren't you clever? Fancy you managing to track me down to the Bell and Goat!'

'The Bell and Goat?' She hadn't been aware of the pub's name!

He smiled at her knowingly. 'It's one of my favourite haunts.'

'Well, I didn't track you down!' Though she felt almost as though she might have. Perhaps, without her knowing it, he had manipulated her into coming here! She rejected the idea. Now she was being fanciful! Even Justin wasn't capable of that!

She glared at him. 'I just happened to stop off here—at random!'

'And did you enjoy your lunch? I noticed you had the ploughman's special. Usually it's very good.'

'It was excellent.'

Tina delivered her reply between clenched teeth. So he had, after all, known she was here all along. Those deceiving grey eyes of his had even registered what was on her plate!

She glared at him, feeling tricked and cheated and as mad as hell. 'By the way, this is my table and I don't recall inviting you to join me.'

Justin simply smiled at her rebuke, then called to the barman and ordered a couple of glasses of lager. 'It's only civil,' he declared irritatingly, 'that I keep you company.'

'It would be more civil if you didn't.'

But Tina kept her tone light, carefully in keeping with his. For though he was making little digs at her she sensed a reassuring lack of malice, even a hint of good humour in his manner. A weekend away with his fiancée discussing wedding arrangements was obviously doing him a power of good. Maybe now was the perfect opportunity, after all, to get him involved in these negotiations he had promised.

Justin sat back in his seat and let his eyes rove over her, over the pink cotton blouse and the simple pink and white striped skirt she was wearing.

'So, how did your interview go?' he enquired.

'It went extremely well.' Then Tina stopped short and glared at him. 'How did you know I had an interview?' she demanded. Good grief, she thought, not only did he know I was coming to the Cotswolds, he also knew the reason why I was coming!

'How come you're so well-informed about my activities?' she wanted to know.

Justin smiled an evasive smile. 'Surely you know I'm always well-informed? And I have particular reason to be well-informed about you. After all, you're about to become one of my employees again.'

'You keep an eye on all your employees, do you?'

'Some more than others.' He was quite untouched by the scathing note in her voice. 'After all, some need watching more than others.'

'Watching or controlling?'

'Perhaps a little of both.'

'So, you're trying to control me, are you? That's why you're keeping tabs on me?' She glared at him. 'Well, maybe I don't want to be controlled.'

'No, you never did. That's what makes it so enjoyable.' He leaned back in his seat, the dark eyes seeming to challenge her. 'I'm really looking forward to having you back in my employ.'

'You mean back in your power. That's what you like, isn't it? Having people in your power.' So, she'd been right after all. 'You're going to torment me and make my life a misery. You're going enjoy yourself a little before you finally get round to firing me.'

'Sounds good to me.' He let his eyes drift over her. 'I always did enjoy tormenting you.'

There was something intensely sexual about the way he said it and about the way his eyes flickered and seemed almost to touch her. And Tina found herself utterly powerless to stop herself responding.

She was aware of a sudden sharp tightening in her stomach. All at once, hungry flames were licking at her loins.

Appalled, she froze. What was happening to her? Once, their sexual chemistry was something she had revelled in, but to feel now what she had just felt was no less than a disgrace.

She glared at him, her blue eyes treating him to one of those ice-cold flickers that never failed to make men back off. But the only effect it had on Justin was to make his smile grow broader.

'I see,' he said, 'that you remember too.'

'I'm afraid I haven't the least idea what you're talking about.' Tina continued to glare at him, her eyes like icicles. Then she brushed aside his innuendo as though she hadn't even understood it. 'Quite frankly, you can torment me all you like—just as long as we manage to come to some understanding about *Scope*.'

There, that was clear enough. Now let's get down to business, she was thinking.

But Justin was not to be directed quite so easily. He watched her for a moment, his dark eyes mysterious. Then he said in a curiously flat tone, 'So, where's the boyfriend? Is he waiting in the wings till you're finished with me?'

Tina took a moment to understand. Then she remembered. He believed she had a thing going with Mike, her photographer friend.

'There's no one waiting in the wings. I happen to have come here on my own.'

'I see. Yes, I suppose I should have guessed that. After all, you always did put your work before romance.' And, though his tone was lightly scathing, Tina had the impression that for some inexplicable reason her answer had pleased him.

She had no desire to please him. With a smile she amended, 'But maybe I'll ring him and tell him to come after all. The Cotswolds is such a romantic spot, it's quite put me in the mood. We could have a sexy Saturday night together and a lazy, romantic Sunday.'

'Indeed you could.' Justin smiled in response. At least, his mouth curled at the corners, though his eyes remained cool.

It was almost as though he disapproved, Tina thought as she looked back at him. But why should he disapprove? What could it possibly matter to him, even if she had a posse of lovers waiting in the wings? Unless, of course, he was vain enough to believe that, after him, there couldn't possibly be any other men in her life.

Yes, that was it. Suddenly she remembered how he had expected her to stay on as his part-time lover after she had found out about Eunice.

What gigantic vanity! She smiled to herself with pleasure. Well, from now on she would miss not a single opportunity to take a swipe at such shameless, misplaced conceit.

It was at that moment that the barman appeared with their lagers. As he laid them on the table, Justin pushed Tina's towards her. 'Drink up,' he told her. 'And don't worry, it's non-alcoholic. I noticed your car outside. I know you're driving.'

So, he had even noticed her car! Tina felt stung with irritation. He had known she was here even before he entered the pub!

He seemed to sense her irritation and proceeded to double it. 'I wouldn't want to be responsible for you drink-driving,' he teased. 'Or, indeed, for spoiling the sexy Saturday night you're planning.

Sex, like driving, tends to be performed better when one's not drunk.'

This time as he smiled there was no holding back in his eyes. And perhaps there hadn't been a moment ago, either, Tina reflected. Perhaps she had just imagined it. It was unlikely, after all, that he gave a damn about her lovers. She found that just a little disappointing.

'But what you were saying about the Cotswolds was quite right,' he told her. 'It is a very romantic place.'

Tina took a mouthful of her lager. 'I suppose that's why you bought a house here?'

'One of the reasons. I wanted a place for weekends. It's good to get out of the city from time to time.'

'It must be.' Tina regarded him over the rim of her lager glass. That was the very reason she'd decided to spend the weekend here. It felt good to leave the pressures of London behind for a while.

She looked into Justin's eyes. 'It must be a fairly new acquisition. You didn't have a house in the Cotswolds in my time.'

As soon as she'd said it, Tina could have bitten out her tongue. What a stupid thing to say. It had sounded almost wistful. As though she harboured fond memories of those best-forgotten days!

'At least, not as far as I recall,' she added, shrugging elaborately and taking a rather large mouthful of her lager. Then she raised her eyes carefully, daring Justin to pick up her *faux pas*.

But he didn't. Clearly, he had no desire to remember those days either. Instead, he said, 'It's a fairly recent acquisition. I bought it just over eighteen months ago.'

'For weekends, you say? How very pleasant. Eunice must enjoy it too.'

Tina felt rather pleased by her light tone as she added that last bit. By introducing Eunice into the conversation so coolly she had neatly dashed any false suspicion she might have provoked in him that she gave a damn about their past. And she'd even managed to use the wretched woman's name for once!

Justin showed no reaction. He picked up his lager and drank. 'Yes, I suppose she does,' he agreed.

Tina watched him through narrowed eyes. She had no desire to talk about Eunice or about his Cotswolds house or any of that. What she wanted to talk about was the future of *Scope*. He was well aware of that, of course, but he was enjoying keeping her on tenterhooks. And, though Tina knew it would be useless to try and twist his arm, perhaps, if she was subtle, she could guide the conversation round.

She leaned casually across the table and fingered her lager glass. 'I couldn't help noticing that Eunice left early. Was there any particular reason?' She smiled an innocent smile. 'I mean any reason why you wanted to be on your own.'

For it had occurred to her that perhaps he had packed Eunice off so that he could have a word with Tina in private. Perhaps, since he and Eunice were spending the weekend together, he'd had second thoughts about Tina coming to the house later on.

But Justin wasn't to be caught out so easily. 'Why? Did you want a word with her?'

'No.'

'I didn't think so. You don't like Eunice, do you?'

Tina was a little taken aback, but she could scarcely deny it. She tilted her chin at him. 'And she doesn't like me.'

'Eunice has nothing against you.' Justin was shaking his head at her. 'The only thing I've ever heard Eunice say about you is that she considers you to be an extremely talented journalist.'

Could that possibly be true? Tina stared at him in amazement. If it was, then Eunice was every bit as devious as her fiancée. Tina suddenly felt out-smarted and at a bit of a disadvantage. Con-sidering the things she'd said about Eunice, she must look a total bitch!

Justin more or less confirmed that as he pro-ceeded to assure her, 'Eunice didn't even notice you were here, as it happens, and I certainly didn't bring your presence to her attention.' He smiled without humour. 'Knowing your penchant for scenes, the last thing I was likely to do was bring you together. I had no desire to see Eunice upset.'

Tina felt like punching him for his smug superi-ority. Or maybe it was for that declaration of support for his fiancée. She didn't like to admit it, but that stuck in her throat.

But she bit back her annoyance and kept her tone pleasant. 'So, why didn't you leave with her? Why did you stay on after she'd gone?' *Do I have to spell it out in words of one syllable?* she was thinking. *I'm tired of chit-chat. I want to get down to business!*

But Justin was enjoying keeping her dangling too much. He leaned back in his seat and narrowed his eyes at her. 'So, your interview went off well. Tell me about it.'

Tina sighed inwardly. 'What do you want to know? It was just a straightforward interview for an article for *Scope*.' Her eyes drifted momentarily to her bag on the seat beside her. Her tape recorder with the interview on it was safely inside it. 'I really can't think it's of any interest to you,' she added.

'I thought you didn't do articles any more? Now that you're an editor.' Justin was totally immune to the impatient entreaty in her eyes.

'I don't normally.' Tina sighed with resignation. 'I don't really have the time, but this was an emergency.' *OK, her eyes were telling him, I'll play along with you. But one way or another I'll pin you down in the end!*

She sat back in her seat. 'One of my freelances let me down—disappeared off to France, leaving me with half an article. The extra information we needed had to be got in a hurry, so I decided to do it myself.'

'That was extremely diligent of you. So, what is this article about?'

Tina sighed again inwardly. Was he going to spin this out forever? But she had no choice but to go along with him. No other strategy would work.

So she told him, 'It's part of a series about couples in the nineties. Every month we feature a different couple who talk about themselves.'

'And the Cotswolds is a rich source of typical nineties couples, is it?'

'They're not all typical. It would be rather boring if they were.' Tina met his sarcasm with a touch of her own. 'They're just a cross-section. Some typical, some not. But all of them are interesting in their own way. The idea is to give as broad a picture as possible of what couples in the nineties are all about.'

'I see.' Justin had picked up his lager glass and was watching her over the top of it, an amused, sarcastic glint in his iron-grey eyes. 'So tell me,' he demanded, lifting one curved black eyebrow, 'what are nineties couples all about?'

'Don't you already know that?' The retort came out before she could stop it. 'After all, you're half of a nineties couple yourself.'

'Am I?'

'I would say so.' Tina's cheeks were flaming.

'In that case,' he invited, 'perhaps you ought to interview me?'

'You mean you and Eunice. All the couples are interviewed together.'

'Surely, in my case, you could make an exception?'

A typical Justin remark! Conceited and arrogant!

Tina ignored it and observed mockingly, 'I wouldn't have thought that was your scene—baring your all to the magazine-reading public.'

'Would I be required to bare my all?'

'You'd be required to be honest.'

Her tone was sharp, but as she caught the smile in his eyes all at once Tina couldn't stop herself from smiling back at him. Disarmed, she thought bleakly, as only Justin could disarm her. And it was a strangely intimate feeling sharing that silly *double entendre* with him. It sent a warm rush of pleasure flooding round her heart.

Fool! she told herself instantly, and added in an even sharper tone, 'There'd be no point in taking part unless you were prepared to be honest. And I suspect you would probably find that rather hard.'

'So, honesty is an essential part of coupledom these days?' Justin laid down his lager glass. 'You've made me curious. Tell me more about this fascinating nineties phenomenon.'

Tina felt a thrust of annoyance at the way her insult had just bounced off him. He didn't care. He simply had no conscience. But she shook off her anger. So, what was new about that? She continued, answering his question, 'Our couples also value openness and all aspects of sharing in their relationships, and they think it's important to have respect for one another. Like I said, they're all different, but they seem to share these basic attitudes.'

Justin was watching her closely, as though he was genuinely interested. And Tina found herself wondering curiously if he shared any of those attitudes.

It seemed unlikely, unless Eunice had worked some miracle—some miracle that she herself had certainly failed to bring off.

In spite of herself, Tina felt a tug of resentment at that thought.

'Openness…sharing…respect for one another.' Justin continued to watch her as he repeated what she'd said. Then all at once he shifted forward a little, so that he was facing her more squarely. 'And what about loyalty? Do they believe in loyalty as well?'

'Loyalty?' Tina had started at the suddenly aggressive way he was confronting her. All at once, there was a look of dark hostility in his eyes. 'Loyalty?' she said again.

'Yes, loyalty. I see you have difficulty with that concept.' His eyes hooked into her like a pair of steel claws. 'But that's not surprising. I should have remembered you always did.'

Tina felt herself blanch. He had the nerve to accuse her when her sins were minuscule in comparison to his!

She glared at him hotly. 'One has to be selective with one's loyalty. Some things—and people—are not worth being loyal to.'

'Oh, you don't have to explain to me.' Justin's tone was cutting, his eyes like sharp knives slashing into her. 'I'm already well-acquainted with your philosophy. The only loyalty you understand is loyalty to Tina Gordon. As long as you can get what you want and look after number one, you don't give a damn about anyone else.'

'About you, you mean? Why should I ever have given a damn about you——?'

But he cut in, 'I'm not talking about me. I'm not talking about the past. To hell with all that! To hell with the past! What I'm talking about is now and how you haven't changed. Still the same old selfish values as before. The same unstinting concern for number one which, to be truthful, I find just a little sickening.'

As he delivered this attack, flames were shooting from his eyes, flames that seemed to turn to ice as they touched her. Tina felt herself draw back as a shiver went through her, her own anger suddenly shrivelling to nothing.

'I don't know what you're talking about,' she said, feeling her scalp prickle.

'Don't you?' Justin's eyes were full of distaste, as though she were some vermin he might squash beneath his shoe. 'What I'm talking about is your readiness—no, your outright enthusiasm—to come to some private arrangement with me that will safeguard your position as features editor of *Scope*. It seems to me that's the only thing in the world you care about.'

Tina shook her head. He'd accused her of this before. 'That's total nonsense, as I keep telling you! It's not just my own job at *Scope* I care about!'

'In that case, no doubt you've told your colleagues all about these negotiations of ours that are supposedly on the cards?' His eyes bored into her. 'Just like you said you would.'

Tina flushed then. 'No, I didn't——'

'And do they know about our proposed meeting this afternoon?'

'No——'

'No, of course they don't! You never intended telling them anything. Secret negotiations, that's what you're good at. Secret negotiations behind your colleagues' backs.' His lips twisted with scorn and distaste as he added, 'Well, there'll be no secret negotiations. I'm going to put a stop to you. And by the time I'm through with you not only will you not be editor of *Scope*, there won't be a damned magazine in all of London that'll touch you with a bargepole!'

There was so much hate in his eyes Tina could scarcely bear to look at him. She felt a thrust of nausea deep inside her, choking her, turning her blood to powder in her veins.

She had to get out of here. She couldn't listen to another word. She reached for her bag on the seat beside her, but her hands were shaking so badly that she spilled the whole lot on the floor. Barely looking at what she was doing, she stuffed everything back in again, then, clutching the bag to her chest, stumbled to her feet.

'Get out of my way.' She pushed her way past Justin. 'Get out of my way and stay out of my way!'

Then she was barging between the tables, heading blindly for the door, oblivious of all around her, sick to her soul.

But she did catch Justin's final comment. 'Go on, run,' he mocked her. 'You won't get far.'

CHAPTER SIX

ONCE outside the pub, Tina stumbled towards the car park. Her heart was thundering like a cataract inside her and her legs felt as flimsy as sheets of paper. How she ever reached the car she had no idea.

But she did, and fell into the driver's seat gratefully, hands trembling as she fumbled in her bag for her car key. She had to get away from here as fast as she could.

She drove till she came to a quiet little lay-by, then pulled over and switched the engine off. Her heart had slowed a little, but it was still pumping fiercely. She leaned back in her seat and breathed deeply for a while.

Justin's threats were still echoing like gunfire in her head. Where had all that hate he had poured out at her come from? She had known that he hated her. But not that much. That was upsetting enough, but what was even more upsetting was the crazy way she had reacted to his outburst.

If any other man in the world had spoken to her like that she'd have picked up his lager and thrown it in his face. But, because it was Justin, she'd fallen apart and ended up fleeing out of the pub like an idiot. He still had this power over her. He could still reduce her heart to ashes.

She felt tears start in her eyes. Where was her famous armour? The armour she had so meticulously gathered around herself to keep herself safe, to shut out danger. What good was it when all it kept out were harmless flies and fell apart at the first encounter with a tiger? It was against tigers that she needed it. Justin was a tiger. And he was clawing her apart, just as he'd promised.

Oh, God, she thought helplessly as the tears brimmed over. What on earth am I going to do?

Well, tears weren't going to help, she told herself impatiently, sniffing loudly and reaching for a tissue from her bag. She blew her nose loudly and dabbed the tears from her cheeks, then checked quickly in the mirror for running mascara. She would go for a drive for a bit and pull herself together. And then she would decide what her plan of action should be.

She picked up her bag, about to drop it on to the back seat. If she was going for a drive, she'd need her map. But then she paused, still holding the bag in mid-air. Something was wrong. The bag felt too light. With a dart of alarm, even before she looked inside, she realised the reason why.

Her tape recorder was missing. She felt a rush of pure panic. This morning's vital interview was recorded on the tape! What on earth could have happened to it?

And then she remembered. When she'd been making her escape from Justin, she'd tipped up her bag and some of her things had fallen out. She hadn't noticed at that time, but her tape recorder must have been one of them.

With a sigh of relief, she turned on the ignition. It was probably still lying where it had fallen. So, the sooner she got back to the pub and claimed it the better.

It was only a short drive back to the Bell and Goat, and as Tina quickly slotted her little blue Panda into the car park she was relieved to see that there was no sign of the white Mercedes. One thing she could definitely do without was another confrontation with Justin!

She dived into the pub and went straight to the table by the window—which was unoccupied, she was greatly relieved to see. But after a couple of minutes' frantic grovelling on the floor she was rapidly concluding that the tape recorder wasn't there.

Then a voice spoke. 'Hey, miss! Are you looking for something? The gentleman found it and took it away.'

Tina staggered to her feet and turned to face the barman who had spoken. 'What gentleman?' she enquired. 'Where did he take it?'

'The gentleman you were with. The one with the white Mercedes. He said you should go and pick it up from his house, but if he doesn't see you he'll return it to your office first thing Monday morning.'

Tina was listening in a state of mingled relief and anger. So her tape recorder wasn't lost. Justin had taken it. And now he expected her to go to his house to collect it.

Damn him! she thought furiously. Why couldn't he just have left it with the barman?

The barman was continuing, 'He said you knew his address, but anyway, it's Beech Hedges, about six miles from here. Turn left out of the pub grounds and keep going till you pass the church. But if you get lost just ask anybody. Everyone round here knows Beech Hedges.'

Tina thanked him, left the pub and walked back to her car. I'm not going, she told herself. I'm definitely not going. I don't need the interview till Monday anyway. So why should I subject myself to further grief?

She climbed into the Panda and switched on the engine. I'm going to look for a place to spend the night, she told herself firmly, and just put the tape recorder and Justin out of my mind. Wild horses couldn't drag me within a mile of his wretched house.

Besides, she thought bitchily, remembering what Justin had said earlier, if I turned up it would only upset Eunice!

No, there's no way I'm going. She spread out her map on the passenger seat. She would turn right out of the pub grounds and go and look for a bed and breakfast.

But something strange happened. Some genie in the steering-wheel seemed to take control as she reached the pub exit. For, as though of its own accord, the little blue Panda turned left.

A few minutes later Tina was turning into the grounds of Beech Hedges and reflecting that it was little wonder everyone in the area knew the house.

It was a magnificent edifice. An eighteenth-century mansion, all turrets and tall chimneys and ivy-clad walls. It looked more like the country seat of some belted earl than the modest weekend retreat she'd been expecting.

Though she'd been foolish to expect that, she told herself sternly. When had Justin ever gone in for modesty?

She rang the brass bell once and it was answered immediately by a middle-aged woman in a neat blue uniform. The help, Tina thought caustically as the woman greeted her with a smile. After all, you couldn't expect Justin to open his front door himself. And certainly not Eunice. She might ruin her fingernails.

Bitchy, she chastised herself. What was getting into her? Why this sudden outbreak of bitchiness against Eunice?

It's just bad humour, she told herself as she smiled back at the housekeeper. And who could blame her for bad humour, the way Justin was giving her the runaround?

'I'm Tina Gordon,' she told the woman. 'I've come to see Mr Marlowe.' Then a thought suddenly occurred to her. Maybe she needn't see him at all. 'He has something of mine,' she elaborated hopefully. 'Maybe he's left it with you in case I called?'

'Yes, he said there was a possibility you might be calling, Miss Gordon.' As the woman nodded, Tina felt a spurt of optimism. But it died a little as the housekeeper stood aside, inviting her to step into the huge mirrored hallway. 'Come in. I'll tell Mr Marlowe you're here.'

'Is that necessary? I mean, couldn't I just wait here? It wouldn't take you a minute to fetch the tape recorder for me.'

Tina remained standing on the doorstep, reluctant to step inside the tiger's lair. But at that precise moment she heard an all too familiar growl.

'Ah, so you got my message. That's good. Come on in. I take it you have come to pick up the tape recorder?'

And why else would she be here? To pay him a social visit? Tina grimaced in response. 'Yes,' she said tightly. 'So may I have it?'

'Of course you may have it.' Justin waved away the housekeeper. 'It's your property after all. Why wouldn't you be able to have it?'

He was in one of those moods of his where he enjoyed tormenting her. As he stood there in the hallway, hands loosely in his trouser pockets, Tina was having no trouble picking up all the signals: the amused tilt of the head, that dark sparkle in his eyes, the way his lips curled mockingly at the corners.

But at least there was no hint of harshness in his expression. The hatred of before that had turned her blood to powder was now, thankfully, nowhere to be seen. Tina was a little ashamed by how relieved she felt at that.

For here she was acting out of character again. If any other man had treated her the way he had earlier, she wouldn't even be considering giving him the time of day, let alone worrying about what kind of mood he was in. She would simply be demanding that he hand back her property.

Why was it that she allowed Justin to disarm her so easily? Well, it was time she put a stop to it. It definitely wasn't healthy.

She straightened her spine. 'Yes, it is my property, so would you mind handing it over to me—immediately, please?'

'Come in and I'll fetch it for you.' Justin was unmoved by her sternness. He continued to look back at her with that amused look in his eyes. 'Since you've come all the way here, you may as well step inside.'

'I needn't have come all the way here.' Tina brushed aside his logic and fixed him with a stony look of censure. 'If you'd left the tape recorder with the barman—which would have been the normal thing to do—I wouldn't have had to make this visit.'

'That's true.' Justin nodded. 'But you might not have realised you'd lost it until you were back in London. That was why I decided to take it under my wing.'

That hadn't occurred to Tina. Perhaps she ought to thank him after all? Perhaps she'd been wrong to assume he'd taken it just to torment her?

She pulled a mildly contrite face, her sternness receding again. 'That was extremely thoughtful of you.' Though she still wasn't totally convinced.

'So, now that we've sorted that out, do come in,' he invited again. 'I can't have my guest standing on the doorstep.'

As he spoke, he stepped to one side, inviting her to enter the huge hall.

'Please don't be shy,' he urged. 'Just for five minutes.'

It wasn't shyness that was making her hesitate, as he very well knew. Tina was hesitating because she was wondering what he was luring her into!

But five minutes couldn't hurt. And there was no point in wrangling. He obviously wasn't going to hand over the tape recorder until she obliged by stepping inside. Besides, Tina had to admit, she was just a tiny bit curious to see the inside of this fabulous house!

Nice, she observed to herself, very nice indeed, as he led her across the hall and through an archway into the drawing-room, where soft-cushioned sofas in faded russets and terracottas and Chinese lamps with huge silk shades created an atmosphere that was both elegant and relaxed.

It didn't look like Eunice's taste, Tina found herself thinking. Eunice would go in for brighter, sharper colours. She found herself feeling oddly pleased that Eunice's hand wasn't evident in the décor.

'Come and meet my guests.' Justin was leading her across the room to where French doors stood open, leading on to a large patio. 'They've just been taking a look at the garden.'

Guests? What was he talking about? She hadn't come to meet his guests!

Tina stopped in her tracks and complained to his back, 'I can only stay for five minutes. I really don't think I should bother. Just give me the tape recorder and I'll be on my way.'

But Justin was already stepping out on to the patio. Either he hadn't heard her or he had chosen totally to ignore her, and Tina had a pretty good idea which of the two it was! On stiff, annoyed strides, she came up behind him and was about to repeat her protest as she joined him outside. But she was too late. A smiling twosome was coming towards them.

It was a girl and a young man, the girl dark-haired and extremely pretty, and she was the first of the two to speak.

'What an absolutely gorgeous garden,' she told Justin. She grinned and held up the plastic bag in her hand. 'I hope you don't mind, but I've taken a couple of cuttings.' Then she turned to Tina. 'Hi,' she said.

'Hi.' Tina smiled back at her, finding her instantly likeable. She was surprised. She hadn't expected to find anyone in Justin's house that she would like. But even the young man with the girl looked decidedly pleasant.

Still, she couldn't suppress a nervous glance past them to the garden. Any minute now, surely, Eunice would appear and that would be the end of this polite little interlude?

But there was no sign of Eunice as Justin took over the proceedings. 'Let me introduce you to my niece,' he was saying to Tina. He gestured to the dark-haired girl. 'This is Victoria.' Then he nodded to the young man. 'And this is Jean-Pierre, Victoria's boyfriend. Meet Tina,' he told them, 'one of the best journalists in London.'

Tina was too busy shaking hands with Victoria and Jean-Pierre to check out the expression that accompanied that compliment. But she suspected he'd probably looked as utterly sincere as he'd sounded. Wasn't he, after all, a master of deceit?

'So, you're a journalist? Are you in magazines, like Uncle Justin?' Victoria's bright brown eyes were full of interest. 'One day, after I've finished my studies, I'd like to get into journalism too.'

'I would thoroughly recommend it. There's no better job.'

So, this is Victoria, Tina was thinking, trying to suppress the sudden sharp jolt of remembrance. She'd totally forgotten that Justin had a niece, but now she remembered going shopping with him three years ago to find a present for Victoria's fifteenth birthday. They'd bought some pop videos, she remembered, and what fun they'd had choosing them.

She glanced at Justin, her heart suddenly full of remembering, and her throat felt so tight it was difficult to breathe. That happy shopping trip suddenly felt like yesterday, but really it had been a lifetime ago. And in the meantime Justin's niece had blossomed into a beautiful young woman. Tina felt oddly touched by that, but at the same time regretful. By comparison, there had been very little blossoming in her own life. In fact, apart from her career, nothing had blossomed at all.

She chased that thought from her. It was inaccurate and maudlin. There was no man in her life, but everything else was rosy. She had good friends and a wonderful family and one day, maybe, she'd fall in love again. In the meantime, she could live very well without it.

'Tell me about what you do.' Victoria had taken her by the arm and was leading her back inside the drawing-room as the two men, chatting together, followed behind. 'Maybe you can give me a couple of career tips.'

To Tina's amazement, there followed the most enjoyable couple of hours. The housekeeper brought tea and buttered scones on a tray and the four of them sat around chatting as though they'd all known each other for years. And as though, Tina reflected privately, she and Justin were the best of friends. Not one single harsh word or look passed between them.

They talked about Paris, Jean-Pierre's home town, though Tina had to admit it wasn't a city she knew well.

'I've only been there once, and then only for the weekend. But I thought it was an incredible place,' she told them. 'I'd love to go again.'

'You must,' Victoria urged her. 'And make sure you tell Justin first. Then we can alert Jean-Pierre's relatives and get them to show you round. No one can show you Paris like a Parisian.'

'I'm sure.'

Tina bit diplomatically into her fruit scone and avoided looking anywhere near Justin. Victoria obviously thought they were on the best of terms. What a wonderful performance they both must be giving!

But though she was smiling to herself sceptically she felt oddly regretful too. Three years ago there would have been no need to put on a performance. Three years ago this scene could have happened for real. And again she had the sensation that time had stolen something from her and left her with a handful of nothing.

But again she chased the feeling from her and chastised herself crossly. Why couldn't she just enjoy this moment for itself, without having to drag in the dark and dreary past? Besides, she was fooling herself. Those days had seemed happy, but that was only because she hadn't known Justin was lying. She hadn't known she was simply being taken for a ride.

It was only as Victoria and Jean-Pierre were getting ready to leave that it suddenly struck Tina that Eunice still hadn't appeared. Even funnier, she hadn't even once come up in the conversation. Where on earth was she? Tina wondered. Was she upstairs with a migraine or something? Had she gone back to London? Oh, well, she told herself, just be grateful for small mercies.

'Where is it you're off to tonight?' Justin was asking Victoria as they all moved through to the hall to say their farewells.

'We're going to see that new Al Pacino movie everyone's raving about.' Victoria kissed her uncle on the cheek, then shook hands with Tina and kissed her too. 'It's been lovely meeting you. I hope we meet again.' Then a moment later she and Jean-Pierre were climbing into Jean-Pierre's battered old Peugeot.

As Justin stood to wave them off, Tina wondered if she ought to walk away. Now that there was no need for him to be polite to her any more, perhaps he would prefer it if she did. But Victoria and Jean-Pierre might think her rude if she disappeared, and she might as well see this charade out to the end. So she just stood where she was, smiling and waving, until the Peugeot finally disappeared from view.

'So, what do you think of my niece?'

As Justin closed the door at last, he turned around and smiled at Tina.

'I like her a lot,' Tina answered honestly. 'I thought she was lovely. A really super girl.' And she felt oddly touched as she was rewarded for her generosity by a look of deep pride in the iron-grey eyes. Justin clearly loved his bright young niece very much. She found herself adding, responding instinctively and unthinkingly to the warmth she suddenly felt flowing from him, 'She's grown up a lot since she was that fifteen-year-old with a passion for U2.'

As soon as she said it, Tina wished she hadn't. He would either respond with a blank look or chastise her with his eyes for presuming to bring up the past like that. For there had been something rather intimate about the remark.

But he neither chastised her nor looked blank. Instead, surprising her, he smiled. 'Indeed she has.' Then he held her eyes. 'Fancy you remembering that.'

I remember it all. Every precious second of it.

The thought went through Tina's head, but she did not say it—though, to her horror, for one foolish moment she'd been tempted.

Am I going crazy? she rebuked herself, snatching her gaze from Justin's. *He'd really be amused if you started coming out with stuff like that.*

Besides, it wasn't true. She didn't remember, she told herself as they made their way across the huge mirrored hallway. She'd forgotten. Completely. It was just thinking of Victoria that had triggered off that long-dead memory.

'We bought them in Oxford Street. The videos, I mean.' As he spoke, Justin's eyes were on her, making her skin prickle. 'I seem to remember,' he added, 'you had a bit of a passion of your own. Didn't we end up buying a couple of Pavarotti tapes for you on the same trip?'

Tina felt her stomach simultaneously lurch and disappear. She stopped in her tracks and turned to look at him. 'You mean to say you remember that?'

She still had those tapes. Hidden at the back of a drawer. She'd never listened to them again after she and Justin had broken up.

The colour had gone from her face as he stood there watching her. All at once, Tina's heart was racing inside her. There was a lump as big as a football in her throat.

'I remember all sorts of things,' Justin said. The dark eyes looked down at her, seeming to wrap all around her, soft as velvet, enfolding her in their depths.

'Oh?'

Once upon a time, Tina had known that look well, and she knew too the rush of feelings it provoked in her. She felt something soften inside her and her eyelids droop a little. Now, she thought, he would reach out and touch her.

He did. He touched her cheek and moved a little closer.

'You might be surprised how much I remember,' he murmured. There was tenderness in his voice and his touch was as soft as gossamer as, very slowly, he caressed her cheek, letting his fingers slide down to brush against her chin, then, tantalisingly, erotically, slide against her throat. Tina was incapable of speech and she could barely even focus as she felt him smile and add a little throatily, 'And right now it's all coming back very clearly.'

She recognised that throaty tone. Something flared inside her. Now, for certain, he would kiss her.

But he did not kiss her immediately. For the space of a heartbeat, he simply gazed down at her, eyes pouring over her like honey. Then she heard him sigh as his free hand reached out towards her, curling round her waist, drawing her against him. Then, making her whole body shiver, he bent to press his lips to hers.

This was how she remembered it. Tenderness and passion. The gentleness of his kiss drove the breath from her body, while the fire behind the gentleness sent flames rushing through her.

Tina clung to him, her whole body sobbing with the wanting of him, filled with the sweet, delicious agony of excitement that only Justin had ever awakened within her. Her skin was on fire. A tempest raged through her heart.

'Oh, Justin!' she moaned, running her fingers through his hair.

His arm around her was tight, holding her like a prisoner, though there could have been no more willing prisoner than Tina at that moment. As his free hand slipped down, firm and hungry to cup her breast, moulding the warm, swelling flesh against his palm, teasing the aching nipple through the thin fabric of her blouse, she was praying that this dizzy moment might never come to an end.

Wantonly, she pressed against him, feeling his hardness thrust against her stomach. Liquid with desire. Aching with her need for him. Suddenly, she was on a roller-coaster, unable to stop.

Justin kissed her face hungrily. Her lips, her cheeks, her eyes. And she kissed him back, her hands roaming over him, delighting in the firm, hard contours of his shoulders, sliding down to press excitedly against his chest.

It was all so familiar. She knew this body so well. And it felt so right, the way he was touching her and kissing her. Right in a way it had never felt with any other man.

You're mine! You belong to me! she found herself singing through her excitement. You've always belonged to me! You could never belong to anyone else!

A sense of giddy triumph filled her. Time had stolen nothing after all! Justin was still hers! She had not been left with nothing! But even as she thought it, her heart soaring with happiness, the cold finger of reality was reaching out to touch her, making her shiver, turning her triumph to dust.

She shivered and drew away, detaching her hands from him as though scorched. She was mad. Justin wasn't hers. He belonged to Eunice.

His eyes showed his surprise as she tore herself free from him. 'What is it?' he demanded, his tone rough and ragged.

'*What is it*?' Tina was almost fainting with horror. Horror at herself, at the way she had behaved. She glared at him, adjusting her blouse, which had become detached from her skirt. 'You dare to ask me "What is it?"! Have you forgotten about Eunice?'

'It would appear we both had.' He smiled lop-sidedly. 'But don't worry, Eunice isn't here.'

'And what difference does that make?' That simply made her more furious. Did he expect her to fall back into his arms again, now that she knew the coast was clear? That was insulting. Tina's blue eyes turned to daggers. 'What do you think I am? I'm getting out of here!'

And though her legs had turned to straw, she turned on her heel gallantly and proceeded to march in as straight a line as she could manage across the hall towards the door.

She pulled the door open and plunged down the stone steps, then she was racing towards her car and collapsing inside. And that was when she realised she'd forgotten her bag.

'I think you'll need this.'

Even before she could find the breath to curse, Justin was standing by the still open door and holding out her bag to her. Tina snatched it without looking at him and rummaged inside for her car key. Then, finding it, she stabbed it into the ignition.

'Get out of my way and let me close the door!' she hissed threateningly, stamping very hard on the gas.

The engine hadn't caught. Tina cursed and tried again, her right foot nervously pumping the accelerator. Then as the engine flickered and stalled she hissed again in frustration. 'How can I possibly start this thing with you standing there staring at me?'

Justin did not move. He continued to lean against the door-frame. She could feel the dark eyes watching her every nervous move. And though she had not once dared to look up at him she could sense his smile as he told her, 'It's not going to start. You've flooded the engine.'

Tina felt like weeping. 'Then I'll just sit here and wait for it to unflood!'

But she didn't. Driven by her nerves, she twisted the key again, pressing hard on the accelerator and simply making matters worse.

'I'll tell you something else. You haven't taken your tape recorder.'

As the engine coughed pathetically, Justin held out his hand to her.

'I think you'd better come back inside again,' he told her. 'What you need is a drink and five minutes to calm down.'

'I'm not coming back inside.'

'Just for five minutes. I think you ought to.'

'Five minutes! That's what you said before and look what happened!' In helpless frustration, Tina turned to look at him at last. 'That's precisely why I don't want to come back inside!'

But the instant she looked at him her heart seemed to ricochet inside her. He was still smiling and holding out his hand towards her. Suddenly, she didn't have the strength to keep on fighting.

'Come on,' Justin said again, very softly.

'I don't know...'

But Tina had already taken his hand and was allowing him to help her out.

'Good girl.'

Still holding her hand, he was leading her away from the car, up the stone steps and back into the mirrored hallway.

A moment later, the front door closed behind them with a click.

CHAPTER SEVEN

'I DON'T know what you think I've come back for, but it's not for what you're thinking.'

Tina delivered this piece of gobbledegook as Justin led her towards the drawing-room, beneath the high sweeping arch at the end of the hall. She slipped her hand from his and took a small step back away from him.

'I just want you to know that,' she added in an attempt to clarify. 'I haven't come back for what you're thinking.'

On the walk from the car she had calmed down a little, but she still felt hopelessly tight and nervous. That was why she wasn't thinking straight and why she was expressing herself so badly. She felt touched by some strange panic. Poised on a knife-edge.

'That's all right, then.' Justin, by contrast, was quite calm. He smiled. 'So, while we're deciding what you're not here for, let's go through to the drawing-room and have a drink.'

As he spoke, he touched her arm lightly with his fingertips, steering her in the direction of the door. And instantly, almost violently, Tina snatched her arm away, as though someone had stuck a knife in her flesh.

It was guilt, she thought miserably, attempting to cover the gesture by turning rapidly and stepping through the doorway by herself. It was guilt for what had so recently passed between them, that sudden, unexpected, shocking intimacy. Guilt that she had allowed it to happen at all and even more guilt that she had enjoyed it so much.

'Whatever it is you plan on not doing, would you prefer not to do it standing up or sitting down?'

As Tina hovered in the middle of the room, Justin addressed her from the doorway. And though she didn't look at him she could guess at the amused smile he was wearing. Unlike her, he quite clearly was not suffering from guilt.

She didn't answer him. Instead, with silent eloquence, she seated herself in the most isolated chair in the room. What had happened before was not going to happen again. She would fight him off with her naked fists if she had to.

Though such melodramatic measures were unlikely to be called for, she reminded herself as she watched him beneath her lashes. One could scarcely say he had pushed himself on her last time. She'd virtually sent him a written invitation.

'I suggest something alcoholic.' He was stepping towards the drinks cabinet, where an array of crystal decanters was glitteringly set out. 'What do you fancy? I have a vintage sherry here that I can thoroughly recommend.'

'Isn't it a bit early for that?' Tina sat back in her armchair and crossed her legs carefully at the ankles. Maybe alcohol wouldn't be terribly wise in her current hyped-up state, she was thinking. 'I think perhaps I might prefer tea.'

'Don't worry, it's not too early. In fact, it's the perfect hour for a sundowner.' As though she hadn't spoken, Justin proceeded to pour two sherries. 'Anyway, this is what you need. Not more tea.'

And how would he know what she needed? Tina scowled at him. Though he was right about the time. It was well after six. She'd had no idea it was so late.

He was coming towards her on silent steps across the carpet, holding out her glass to her with a smile. He even moves like a tiger, she thought. Graceful and predatory. Then, instantly, she wished she hadn't thought it as excitement flared hotly in the pit of her stomach. The last thing she should be doing was having thoughts like that!

Justin handed her her glass—which in her anxiety she virtually snatched from him, terrified that their fingers might accidentally touch. I'm behaving like a maniac, she thought.

'Cheers!' Justin raised his glass and took a mouthful of his sherry. He had come to a stop only a foot away from her chair.

'Cheers!' Tina responded, still fighting to avoid looking at him, her gaze fixed somewhere between his shoes and his knees. Was he going to continue standing there, she wondered in wretched annoyance, and reduce her to a total nervous wreck?

But he was turning away and seating himself on a nearby sofa, looking relaxed as he stretched his long legs out in front of him. Tina stared at his shoes, her misery growing. She should never have come back inside. In fact, she should never have come in the first place. Coming here to his house had been her big mistake.

And the way he was watching her from his seat on the sofa, with that lightly amused smile curling round his lips, it was as though he knew precisely what she was thinking. And was enjoying every second of her discomfort.

It was up to Tina to break the silence. He'd be quite happy to let her stew. So she took a deep breath and finally, looking into his face, told him, 'The only reason I came back was to pick up my tape recorder.'

'No other reason?'

'Definitely not.' She snapped her answer at him. What did he take her for?

But what he had on his mind wasn't quite what she was thinking.

'That's not like you to waste such a golden opportunity.' He paused and smiled a smile of pure wickedness. 'After all, you had me nicely softened up. So to speak.'

Tina understood at once. So, that was what he thought she'd been doing! Trying to soften him up—so to speak—in order to pursue their negotiations!

For a moment she was undecided whether or not to put him right. It might be better for him to believe that her wild abandon had been calculated, rather than to know the truth—that it had been sheer uncontrollable passion!

But then she found herself remembering the way he'd looked at her in the pub when he'd accused her of only ever being out for her own interests, and, though she didn't really give a damn, she found herself saying, 'You already said the negotiations were off. And anyway, as it happens, I've changed my mind. I've decided it would be a mistake for us to try to negotiate.'

She could see that she had surprised him and there was satisfaction in that. Up until now she'd had the feeling that he'd second-guessed her every move.

'Oh?' he queried, one jet-black eyebrow lifting. 'And why have you decided that?'

'Because you quite clearly suspect my motives. You think all I care about is my own job.'

'And you're saying I'm wrong?'

'I've always said it. But you, for your own reasons, apparently choose not to believe me.'

'For my own reasons?' Justin smiled a cynical smile. 'You make it sound as though I've invented my own reasons.'

'I suspect that wouldn't be beyond you.'

He hated her enough. And now, it occurred to her, he probably despised her doubly for the way she had so easily fallen into his arms, in spite of knowing he was soon to be married to another woman.

Tina felt a twist inside her. Maybe she deserved his contempt, for in truth, when he'd kissed her, she hadn't even thought about Eunice. He'd felt like hers. She'd forgotten he was promised to another.

She shivered deep inside. How he must have enjoyed her capitulation.

Her eyes flicked him a harsh look. 'You clearly enjoy thinking badly of me. Well, go on, think as badly of me as you like.'

'I will.' Justin swirled the pale sherry in his glass as he regarded her carefully through narrowed dark eyes. 'You see, I know you so well. That's the trouble. Nobody knows you as well as I do.' He let his gaze travel over her, sensuously, unhurriedly, his eyes flickering with a mixture of sexual provocation and contempt. 'Deny it if you can. No one knows you like I do.'

His eyes were making her flesh tingle, though Tina was trying with all her strength to ignore that dark, flickering look in his eyes. But how could she ignore it when the memory of his kiss continued to smoulder like hot cinders on her lips?

She could feel the tension within her that had briefly slackened start to cut like a snare again. Her fingers were tight around the glass in her hand as she told him, 'You don't know me. You only think you do.'

'I only think so, do I?' His eyes burned through her. 'Believe me, I know every beautiful, treacherous inch of you. I know you inside out. I could draw a map.'

Tina licked her dry lips. It was true, she was thinking. No man had ever known her as intimately as he had. He had known her with his hands and his lips and his body. And she had loved every minute of being so thoroughly well-known. She felt a tingle creep round her thighs and a sudden tight-ening in her stomach.

And it was at that precise moment that there was a sudden movement in the drawing-room doorway. Tina's eyes spun round guiltily. Eunice, she thought in panic.

But it wasn't Eunice. It was the blue-uniformed housekeeper.

'Excuse me, sir,' the woman was saying as Tina attempted to gather her shattered nerves. 'What are the arrangements for dinner this evening?'

Justin turned to address her. 'As you've probably gathered, Victoria and Jean-Pierre have gone back to London. So don't bother about dinner. I think I'll eat out. You can have the rest of the evening off.'

Then, as the woman thanked him and disap-peared, he turned once more to Tina. 'Perhaps you'd like to join me?' he suggested.

'You mean you and Eunice?'

Tina's heart was still thumping from that guilty, nervous start when the housekeeper had appeared in the doorway. And no wonder she'd jumped guiltily. That had been a dangerous flirtation.

Justin was watching her. 'No,' he corrected her. 'Not me and Eunice. Just me.'

'Isn't Eunice coming back, then?'

'No. She's gone back to London.'

'Oh.'

Tina hesitated, not sure what to say, hating the way her stomach was twisting inside her. It was quite disgraceful, but the thought of having dinner alone with him had filled her with a bright warm glow of anticipation. Just for an instant, she'd felt horribly tempted to say yes.

But she shook off the temptation. 'Sorry,' she said. 'I can't.'

'You have other arrangements?'

'Yes. As a matter of fact, I have.'

'Of course. Your boyfriend.' Justin nodded, remembering, and sat back against the cushions of the sofa. 'I wouldn't want to keep you from your sexy Saturday night.'

Tina had entirely forgotten about that total fiction about Mike, but she felt grateful to Justin now for having reminded her. Just as she'd been about to sink, he'd conveniently thrown her a lifeline.

She smiled a fond smile that she hoped looked convincing. 'I'm glad he's coming up. I suddenly realised I was missing him.'

'Then I'm glad for you too.' Justin regarded her coolly. Clearly, he wasn't interested in these boring details of her life. Or else, Tina thought, it really did bug him that she apparently had had no trouble replacing him with another man.

Just in case she was right about that and recalling her earlier promise to herself, she added, 'Not a lot of people know it, but Mike and I have been together for quite a while.' She rather hoped this additional piece of fiction would get up his nose.

'Really? Is that a fact?' Justin's tone was dismissive. It seemed that her little invention hadn't got up his nose at all. And, like before, Tina felt a little disappointed that, after all, she had misjudged him. He didn't give a tinker's damn about her love life.

For some reason that made her think about his.

'How come,' she asked, suddenly genuinely wanting to know, 'Eunice isn't spending the weekend here with you?'

'She had work to do, I expect.' He drained his sherry and laid the empty glass down on a nearby table. 'Eunice and I not infrequently spend our weekends apart.'

'Really?'

Tina watched him closely as he delivered this piece of information, noting that he did not look even remotely broken-hearted. To her shame, that rather pleased her, until she remembered—Justin had always liked his freedom, his little dalliances on the side, but in the end he always went back to Eunice.

She felt a coldness touch her. She would never be his dalliance again.

He was watching her, smiling amusedly, as he asked her, 'So, how does that fit into your couples in the nineties picture?'

'Spending time apart? It's definitely not typical.' As no more was infidelity, she reflected to herself. 'Most couples we've spoken to believe it's important to spend time together.'

'So, that makes both of us untypical. After all,' he reminded her, 'it was your original intention to spend the weekend alone too.'

He was right, that was what she'd said, but Tina found herself frowning at him. 'You mean Mike and I are like you and Eunice? Oh, no!' she protested. 'Definitely not!'

The thought appalled her. If she really had a relationship she most emphatically would not want it to be like that. There was genuine emotion in her voice as she went on to tell him, describing the sort of relationship she would one day like to have. 'We're together whenever we can be. We hate it when we're apart. We're two halves of a whole, not two people who occasionally get together.'

Justin raised one dark eyebrow. 'So, it's serious, then?' he put to her.

'Oh, yes, it's serious.'

'That's good. I'm happy for you. I don't know Mike well. I've only met him a couple of times. But he seems like a nice chap. I hope you'll both be very happy.'

'Thank you.'

Tina accepted the false good wishes as though he'd meant them. Which he hadn't of course. Happiness was the last thing he really wished her. But at least, she reflected, the introduction of Mike into the conversation had had the desired effect of cooling the atmosphere between them. There was definitely no risk now of any recurrence of that dangerous flirtation. She ought to get out of here while the going was good.

She glanced at her watch. 'I think I ought to be on my way. I still have to find a place to stay tonight.' She picked up her sherry glass to drain it quickly. 'And, of course,' she added, 'I've got to meet Mike.'

'As you wish. I'll see you out, then.' Before Tina had even finished her sherry, Justin was rising to his feet and leading her to the door. A couple of minutes later she was climbing into the Panda, while he stood watching her at the foot of the stone steps. Good, she told herself. I've escaped.

As she turned the ignition, the engine caught, then died. Oh, no, she suddenly panicked, I'm going to be stuck here after all!

But the second time she tried the engine roared into life. 'Thank heavens,' she breathed as Justin smiled and gave the thumbs up. And a moment later, with a brief wave, she was heading off down the drive. She sighed with relief as she turned out on to the road. She'd escaped from the tiger's lair in one piece after all!

But deep inside her, though she tried very hard to ignore it, there was one tiny treacherous corner of her heart that was bitterly disappointed that the car had failed to stall...

Less than five miles down the road she was to get her come-uppance. As she stopped at a road junction the Panda's engine cut out and, despite all her efforts, refused point-blank to restart.

Tina cursed. 'How could you?' She banged her fist down on the steering-wheel. 'Perverse machine!' she seethed. 'It's no good stalling now!'

But the little car was deaf and unrepentant. It just stood there and refused to produce even so much as a whimper. It was obvious the two of them were going nowhere fast.

Tina climbed out in dismay, resisting the urge to thump the bonnet. Now she would have to find a phone box and track down a mechanic to come to her rescue. Not the easiest job in the world at seven o'clock on a Saturday night.

It took her thirty minutes to find a phone box, then another ten to locate a garage that answered. As she did her best to describe where exactly the car was abandoned, the mechanic told her, 'I'll be there in about an hour.'

An hour! Tina almost felt like weeping with frustration. What a total disaster this day was turning out to be. But she bit her lip and told the man, 'Thank you. I'm ever so grateful.' Then, in a thoroughly black humour, she set out on the trudge back to the car. Her feet were aching, she had a piercing stitch in her side and her poor neglected stomach was grinding with hunger by the time she hobbled round the corner to where she'd left the car.

But in an instant, like magic, all her woes were forgotten as her eyes alighted on the very last sight she'd been expecting to see.

For neatly parked behind the disgraced Panda was a very large gleaming white Mercedes. And seated behind the wheel, smiling at her, was Justin.

'Trouble, I see.' He was climbing out of the Mercedes. 'I'd have had a go at fixing it if you hadn't locked it.'

Tina was trying very hard not to grin from ear to ear. Coming round that corner and suddenly seeing him had felt a bit like winning the National Lottery.

'I don't suppose I need have bothered,' she agreed, trying to sound casual. 'In the state it's in it's not worth stealing.'

'So, what's wrong with it? Refusing to start again?'

Tina nodded. 'It just died on me. Since then, not a whimper.'

Justin had come to stand before her. He glanced down at her flushed face. 'Well, I don't know where you've been, but it's certainly brought the roses to your cheeks.'

'I've walked miles.' Tina scowled to hide the blush that rose up. The way he was looking at her was most disconcerting. 'But at least,' she added, 'I found a mechanic. He said he'd be here in about an hour.' She glanced at her watch. 'Well, about forty minutes now.'

'Forty minutes? I can have a chap here in five. Come with me. Let me give him a ring right now.'

He led the way back to the Mercedes and reached inside for the car phone. 'Take a seat,' he told Tina, waving to the passenger door. 'You look as though you could do with taking the weight off your feet.'

Tina did as she was told and sank gratefully into the passenger seat, though to be honest her feet weren't aching any more and the stitch in her side had miraculously vanished. But she felt oddly shaky and the interior of the Mercedes smelt so nice. It smelt luxuriously of expensive leather, and of Justin.

She breathed in the heady mixture and watched him as he spoke on the phone. This is fate, she was thinking. This was obviously meant to happen. Though why she was thinking that, and what she meant by it, she wasn't certain.

Justin was bending down to talk to her through the open driver's window. 'My man Tim will be here in a couple of minutes. Give me the number of the guy you called and I'll ring and tell him not to bother.'

Luckily, Tina had written the number down on a piece of paper she'd found in the phone box. She slipped it from her bag and handed it to Justin. 'I think he'll be relieved,' she told him. 'He didn't sound too keen to come.'

'You were right. He was relieved,' Justin agreed a minute later as he replaced the car phone inside the car. 'Now give me your car key,' he told her, holding out his hand. 'I'll leave it in the exhaust for Tim to find.' He paused. 'Have you got anything in the boot you're going to need?'

Tina had quite forgotten. 'An overnight bag,' she told him, blushing foolishly as she handed over the car key. Why on earth should an overnight bag make her blush?

A couple of seconds later Justin was sliding into the driver's seat beside her. 'No need for us to hang around,' he told her, switching on the engine. 'I've told Tim to give me a ring once he's found out what the problem is. And in the meantime you and I are going to go and have some dinner.'

As they shot away from the side of the road, he handed her the car phone. 'Phone Mike,' he instructed her, 'and cancel your date.'

Tina blushed to her hair roots. She'd quite forgotten about that lie. Without looking at him, she muttered, 'Actually, that's already been cancelled.' Then she bit her lip guiltily. She shouldn't have done that. She ought to have used her date with Mike as a means of escape.

But she didn't want to escape. And there was no point in trying to. No point at all. This was definitely fate.

Justin took her to a restaurant out in the country, a cosy little place with flickering candles on the tables.

'It's new,' he told her as they left the Mercedes outside and crossed a pretty courtyard bright with potted geraniums. 'This is the first time I've tried it. I'm told it's very good.'

It certainly looked good, Tina decided as they were shown to a corner table and a waiter brought them their menus. The décor was lovely, with lots of potted plants everywhere, and there were some mouth-watering smells drifting from the kitchen.

Yet she couldn't help reflecting that there was surely some significance in the fact that he'd brought her to a place where no one knew him. No doubt at his usual haunts eyebrows would have been raised at the sight of him accompanying a woman

other than his fiancée. And quite clearly that was
something he wished to avoid.

It was foolish, but she felt a dart of annoyance
at that. Even a tiny twinge of hurt. It was just like
in the past when he'd always insisted on being discreet. She'd always been kept hidden, a guilty secret,
never allowed into the mainstream of his life. Only
Eunice was considered good enough for that.

'What takes your fancy?' He was watching her
over the top of the menu. 'Have you decided what
you'd like to eat?'

'The smoked salmon.' It was the first thing Tina's
eye had alighted on. Lost in these thoughts, she
hadn't really been looking at the menu. She ran her
eye quickly down the list of entrées now and added,
'And the veal fricassee for the main course sounds
nice.'

She was being stupid, she told herself. What did
she care where he had brought her or what his
reasons for doing so were? This dinner had no significance. It had just sort of happened. He was at
a loose end and possibly it had amused him to call
her bluff over her supposed date with Mike. And
as for all that fate stuff...well, she'd been out of
her head!

'I think I'll have the salmon, too, and roast
chicken to follow.' As the waiter arrived at their
table, Justin gave him their order. 'And throw in
a bottle of your best Chablis,' he added. Then, as
the waiter moved away, he turned back to Tina.
'Let's make a deal.' He winked across at her. 'I
won't drink more than my fair share of the Chablis

if you'll agree to steer clear of controversial sub-
jects for the evening. Let's try to pretend that we're
just old friends with no particular axes to grind.'

'OK by me.' Tina nodded agreeably, carefully ignoring the way her heart had squeezed inside her.
'Just old friends', he'd said, and it had sounded
piercingly poignant. Though that was silly, she told
herself. They'd never been friends. And, though
she hadn't always been aware of it, there'd always
been axes to grind.

But she pushed these thoughts away and stood
by their deal. Not once did she mention *Scope* or
anything related to the take-over. Oddly enough,
as she began to relax, she didn't even feel the need
to.

'I envy you,' she told Justin as she finished off
her veal, 'having your weekend place in the country.
Sometimes it does one good to get out of London
for a while.'

Justin agreed. 'It was a luxury at first, but now
it's become a necessity. As soon as Friday evening
comes, I can't wait to take off here.'

'I suppose I shouldn't be surprised.' Tina took
another mouthful of her wine. 'I seem to remember you always had a hankering for wide open
spaces. I remember we used to go for runs in the
country quite often.'

She hesitated a little awkwardly as she finished
the sentence. Ought she to be making such references to the past? But she reassured herself. Why
not? That was what old friends did.

And Justin didn't seem to mind. Instead, he smiled at her. 'We used to go to a little restaurant near Chatham a lot. Remember?'

Tina laughed. 'The one with the parrot that used to whistle at all the girls.'

'And when anyone tried to leave it used to shout out, "Stop that man! He hasn't paid his bill!"' Justin shook his head and laughed. 'We had some good times there. I wonder whatever happened to that place? I wonder if it's still going?'

'I'll bet the parrot's still going. It's probably running the place these days.'

Tina's tone was still light, but her heart had shifted helplessly at that throwaway remark about the good times they'd had. They hadn't just been good times. They'd been the best times of her life.

And tonight, too, she reflected, had been almost like those good times. It had felt wonderful to be with him, so relaxed and easy. She'd never realised before how much she missed evenings like this. For there'd been no evenings quite like this, with this special magic, since Justin. She'd never dwelt on it before, but now that seemed impossibly sad.

Justin was watching her and responding to her remark about the parrot.

'You're right, it probably is running the restaurant these days.' Suddenly, his expression had grown more serious. 'I wouldn't mind going back to Chatham one day to find out.'

With Eunice, no doubt. Tina felt her heart plummeting inside her. It was an effort to keep the smile on her face. She glanced down at the tablecloth to hide the emotions she feared revealing, then, changing the subject, laid down her cutlery and pushed her plate away.

'That was absolutely delicious, but I couldn't eat another thing.'

'Not even a small dessert?'

'No, I couldn't. Really. I think I'll even skip coffee, if you don't mind.'

Suddenly, she was nervous about prolonging this intimate situation. It was stirring up emotions she didn't want to feel. All of a sudden she felt vulnerable. She just wanted to get away.

Justin didn't argue with her. 'OK,' he agreed. He smiled a strangely sober smile. 'If that's what you want, I'll get the bill.'

Less than ten minutes later they were leaving the restaurant. In the meantime, Tina had barely spoken another word. She felt all tight and awkward, her whole body aching from the effort of holding back her feelings. And she was painfully aware of every move Justin made. Every gesture. Every glance. Almost every beat of his heart. As though she were joined to him, body and soul, by some invisible cord.

It was as they were crossing the courtyard that led to the car park that Justin suddenly reached out and caught hold of her hand.

'I've enjoyed this evening,' he said. 'It's been very special.'

It was crazy, but at the touch of him Tina felt tears well up. I can't cope with this, she thought helplessly. Please don't let him be nice to me. It would be so much easier to cope with if he started being nasty. She stared hard at the ground, unable to speak.

But worse was to come. As they reached the car, Justin suddenly swung round to catch hold of her other hand. There was an almost fierce look in his eyes as he told her, 'You'll stay the night at my place. I won't hear any arguments. I'll get Mrs Rowlandson, my housekeeper, to prepare the spare room.'

Tina blinked, feeling thrown. She'd been so caught up in the evening that she'd entirely forgotten that she hadn't found a place to stay yet. But she couldn't stay at Justin's. She began to shake her head.

'I think it would be better if I——'

'Nonsense,' he interrupted. 'Tim's going to bring round your car when he's fixed it in the morning. It makes sense for you to stay with me. Besides,' he added as she was about to protest again, 'I want you to stay. I want you under the same roof as me.' Gently, he drew her closer, so that their two bodies were almost touching. 'Tonight, any other arrangement just wouldn't feel right.'

Tina could scarcely breathe for the emotions that filled her. She looked up into his face with helpless longing. He's right, she thought, though she didn't say it. Any other arrangement just wouldn't feel right.

He was still holding her there, only a bee's breath away from him. Tina fancied she could hear the steady beat of his heart. Her own heart seemed to have frozen into a dreamy stillness.

And then he said, his eyes darkening as he looked at her, 'It's good to be like this with you. If only you knew how much I've missed you.'

For a long time he looked at her, making her heart crack in pieces. And then, very softly, he drew her into his arms and kissed her.

It was the softest of kisses. And then he simply held her. Tightly, yet gently, as though she were infinitely precious.

Then he kissed her hair softly. 'Let's go,' he said. He pulled open the passenger door and deposited her inside. A moment later he was climbing in the other side.

Tina felt as though she was floating as they drove back to the house in silence. For there was no need for words. Their happiness glowed like a torch between them.

We've found each other again, she kept thinking over and over. For suddenly it was as though the past three years had never been.

They parked the car and climbed the stone steps to the house together. What was going to happen now? Tina wondered dizzily as, still holding her hand, Justin pushed the front door open. One thing was for sure. She would never let him go again.

But they had barely stepped inside the hallway when they both froze in their tracks.

'Welcome home,' said a voice like a pickaxe.

Walking towards them across the hall was Eunice.

CHAPTER EIGHT

TINA felt herself turn to stone as a sense of horror rushed through her. Eunice! What was Eunice doing here? And she just stood there helplessly, waiting to be devoured, as the red-haired fury descended upon her.

But Justin was stepping forward to stand almost protectively in front of her. He faced his fiancée calmly. 'When did you get back, Eunice?'

'Not a moment too soon, it would seem, by the looks of things!' Eunice's sharp green eyes were as hard as flintstones. Every reed-thin inch of her was bristling with fury. 'It looks as though I got here just in time!'

'Eunice, calm down.' Justin's tone was controlled, though Tina could sense he was secretly fuming. 'Let's not have a scene.' His tone was a warning. It was clear that he would not stand for a scene.

Then he turned to Tina, who had remained rooted to the spot, her stomach churning like a cement mixer inside her. 'I think it's better if we go and find a hotel for you. Come.' He touched her arm lightly. 'Let's go.'

Tina did as she was told. She felt like a zombie. Her brain had turned to putty and her limbs were as numb as cardboard. She was rather grateful to have someone to do her thinking for her. At that moment she was quite incapable of doing it for herself.

But before she was quite through the door Eunice was turning on her. 'That's right, tramp. Get out of here! Get out and stay out! Don't ever dare set foot in this house again!'

As Tina blanched, she continued to spit her venom. 'I already warned you once to keep your hands off my man. You should have listened. I won't warn you again!'

Overcome with nausea, Tina staggered outside. 'Let me out of here!' she almost sobbed. And though she was aware of Justin rebuking Eunice before he followed her outside she did not hang around to listen. On legs that felt like straw she was fleeing towards the car.

'I'm sorry about that. That should never have happened.'

That was the extent of their conversation over the next ten minutes as Justin drove her to a nearby hotel.

You're right, Tina thought. It should never have happened. I should never have been there in the first place. You should never have taken me. But she didn't say anything. She felt incapable of speaking. And anyway, she thought sickly, what would be the point?

So she just sat silent, staring unseeingly through the windscreen, her hands clenched into tight, hard fists in her lap, praying for this nightmare to be over. All she wanted now was finally to be alone. Suddenly, being with Justin was unbearable.

He found a two-star hotel with a sign declaring vacancies. 'I hope this'll be OK,' he said, climbing out and taking her overnight bag from the back.

'It'll be fine.'

Personally, Tina would have settled for something more modest. All she wanted was a bed where she could lay her head and a room that she could lock herself inside. Privacy, not comfort, was all she cared about right now.

She reached out to take her bag from him as Justin began to lead her to the door. 'I won't need your help. I can check in by myself.' She did not even so much as glance at him as she spoke. Then she found herself saying, 'You'd better get back to Eunice.'

He seemed to release the bag reluctantly and Tina could feel his eyes watching her. Then he said, 'I'll ring you tomorrow. We have to talk. In the meantime, just try to get a good night's sleep.'

'I will.' Tina was turning away abruptly. Suddenly, she couldn't wait to put some distance between them. Then in the doorway she half turned. 'Oh, by the way, don't bother ringing.' Before he could answer, she had disappeared inside.

The formalities at the reception desk were mercifully brief. Less than ten minutes later Tina was ensconced in her room. She sank down on to the bed, lay back and closed her eyes. She felt sick with misery and humiliation.

Eunice had called her a tramp and that was precisely what she felt like. Used and cheap and deeply ashamed of herself. For, as much as she disliked Eunice, she couldn't blame her for what had happened. Eunice was Justin's fiancée. She had a perfect right to be upset when she found her future husband with another woman. It was a hard thing to admit, but she had every right in the world.

No, the one to blame for that sickening scene wasn't Eunice, it was Justin, for taking Tina there, and Tina herself for going. For she had known the situation. That he was engaged to be married. Did she have no shame? What had she been thinking of?

A tear slid from beneath her eyelid and traced the curve of her cheek, settling like a drop of crystal against her earlobe. It was all just like before. She was being humiliated all over again, being made to play the part of the other woman. Only this time she had no excuse. This time she'd known the score. This time she'd walked in with her eyes wide open.

Yet how Justin must despise her to have subjected her to that—for he must have known there was a risk that Eunice might come back. And still he had taken her there. He had even insisted. He must hate her even more than she had believed.

Tina clenched her fists tight. But she could learn to live with that. It was tonight's other revelation she would have trouble learning to live with.

For there was no denying it. It had happened in the restaurant car park, during those few blissful moments when Justin had held her close to him and all the years spent apart had seemed to fall away. She'd suddenly realised something she'd perhaps secretly always known. She'd understood why it was that she'd never fallen in love again, why there'd been no man in her life for so long and why she'd suspected there never would be.

She still loved Justin. She'd never stopped loving him. And, no matter what he ever did to her, she would go on loving him forever.

Tina closed her eyes and wept. Surely this was more punishment than she deserved? To love Justin, without hope, for the rest of her life. Tina barely slept that night and she woke early next morning, red-eyed and heavy inside with grief. And suddenly all she wanted was to get back to London.

But then she remembered. What about her car? She couldn't go anywhere until she got her car back. And getting that back, alas, meant contacting Justin.

She'd taken the precaution of taking the phone in her room off the hook last night, just in case he took it into his head to call her. He was the last person she wanted to speak to. In fact she never wanted to speak to him again. Not now. Not ever.

It was when she went down for breakfast that she was told that he had phoned.

'He left a message,' the elderly woman behind the reception desk told her. She reached for the note she had filed away in Tina's key space and handed it to her. 'Here,' she said.

Tina unfolded the note with a sense of trepidation. What if he was suggesting that she go round to the house to collect the car? She would refuse, of course. But that would mean she would have to call him. Her stomach turned over sickly at the thought.

But she needn't have worried. The note laid her fears to rest. The car, it said, would be delivered to the hotel by ten-thirty. The mechanical problem had been fixed.

Good, Tina thought. Now she could get straight back to London and start pretending that this ghastly weekend had never happened. At least she wasn't going to have to confront Justin again.

Tina was up in her room, gathering her few things together, when just after ten, the receptionist rang.

'Your car's here,' she told Tina. 'A young man's just brought it round.'

'Tell him to wait. I'll be down in a minute.'

Tina grabbed her overnight bag and the rest of her things. She would give the young man a cheque for the work that had been done and then she'd be off out of here like a rocket. She'd already paid her hotel bill. There was nothing to keep her.

There was no one in Reception, apart from the elderly receptionist. The old lady nodded towards the front door. 'He's waiting outside.'

'Thanks.' Tina smiled at her and headed for the door. And she felt a lift of sheer relief as she stepped outside and saw her battered old Panda waiting by the kerbside.

But that moment of relief was destined to be brief. To her astonishment and dismay, the driver's door was opening and Justin was climbing out to stand before her.

'You!' She couldn't believe it. 'The receptionist said a young man. I was expecting to see someone from the garage!'

'Sorry to disappoint you.' Justin tossed her a smile, but it was an oddly guarded smile that never reached his eyes. Then he nodded towards the passenger door, taking her bag as he did so. 'I know it's your car, but I'm going to do the driving. Get in,' he told her. And with that he dumped her bag in the back.

Tina didn't budge a centimetre. 'I'm not going anywhere with you.' She held out her hand to him. 'Give me the key. Immediately.'

She might as well have spoken to the tarmac. He was already climbing back into the driver's seat. A moment later the little Panda's engine burst into life and he was releasing the handbrake and slipping into first gear.

'What the devil do you think you're doing?' Tina toyed with the notion of snatching open the driver's door and ejecting him forcibly. It was a nice idea. But perhaps a little fanciful. So she snatched the passenger door open instead and stuck her head inside. 'Get out of my car. This instant!' she demanded. 'Just give me the bill for the repairs and then kindly disappear!'

Justin's reaction was so fast she barely registered what happened next. All she knew was that ap-

proximately a millisecond later she was sitting in
the passenger seat with her safety belt fastened and
they were heading off at a brisk speed down the
road.

'The bill's in the glove compartment,' Justin told
her with a half-smile. 'I would have paid it but I
knew you'd only make a fuss.'

'Make a fuss?' Tina was quite breathless. 'You
really have a nerve!' She glared at him. 'Where the
devil do you think you're taking me?'

'We have to talk. I'm taking you to my place.'

'*Your* place!' The exclamation was a screech of
pure horror. 'I'm not going to your place!' Tina
reached for the door-handle. 'Let me out of here
this instant!'

'Calm down. Eunice isn't there.' Justin reached
across quickly and detached her panic-stricken hand
from the handle. 'Now just relax for a couple of
minutes and try not to get us killed.'

Relax! That was a tall order. Tina sat back mu-
tinously in her seat, feeling a million different emotions seething inside her. What monstrous game was
he playing, kidnapping her like this? And in her
own car! That was the ultimate affront!

She scowled at him as he made a less than perfect
gear change. 'Easy on the clutch!' she snapped at
him. 'Remember this isn't a Mercedes!'

He smiled at that. 'I'll try to remember.' Then
he glanced round quickly at her still flushed face.
'Keep cool. We're nearly there.' And as their eyes
met and held it suddenly struck Tina how tired he

was looking. As though, like her, he hadn't slept much last night.

Though for entirely different reasons, of course. She realised that. He certainly hadn't wept all night in despair. She felt a twist deep inside her and hurriedly dropped her gaze away.

It seemed that in no time they were drawing up outside the house. As they climbed out of the car, Justin slipped the key into his pocket. 'Just in case you think of trying to escape,' he told her, 'before I've finished telling you all I have to say.'

Tina hid her alarm. She already felt like escaping. What was all this about? Why had he brought her here? What on earth was he going to tell her? she was wondering. Fear and confusion and anger seethed inside her. But what she was trying hardest not to do was hope.

He led her across the hall and into the sunlit drawing-room and bade her sit down on one of the terracotta-coloured armchairs. Tina sat down gratefully, for her legs felt like paper. Her hands gripped the chair-arms. 'Well?' she said.

Justin had remained standing a few feet away from her. He looked down at her for a moment, a tall, still figure in a plain white shirt and light grey trousers. There was something oddly shuttered about the expression on his face.

Then he said, shifting slightly, 'The first thing I want to tell you is that everything's over between me and Eunice.'

Tina froze in her seat. Her eyes were fixed on him, but she could not speak.

'She's gone back to London. She won't ever be coming back here. In fact, she and I will not be seeing each other again.'

At last, Tina found her tongue. 'I don't believe you.' She could feel her nails digging into the chair-arms like talons. 'You've just had a fight, that's all. She was angry about last night. But I'm sure once you've explained to her that that was really nothing—I mean, that there's nothing going on between me and you—you'll be able to patch things up again.'

Justin had taken a step towards her as she'd poured out this nervous denial and she could feel her heart thumping like a jackhammer inside her.

Why was he subjecting her to all these lies? For there was no way she believed a single word of it. Had he brought her here just to play out some cruel charade?

But then he spoke again. 'What happened last night wasn't nothing.' The dark eyes bored into her, their expression fierce and urgent. 'And there'll be no reconciliation between me and Eunice. Of that I can assure you absolutely. The truth is it's been over between us for quite a while.'

That look in his eyes was tearing Tina to pieces. 'How can you say that? You can't seriously expect me to believe it.' As she clung to the chair-arms, the room was spinning round her. 'Just the other day everyone was talking about an imminent wedding. You were talking about it yourself.'

'No, I wasn't, because there was never going to be a wedding. I remember you talking about it, and

I know lots of other people were, but you were all talking about something that was never going to happen.'

Tina looked back at him blankly. This was outrageous. 'Excuse me,' she said. 'I'm afraid you'll have to explain.'

'Yes, I think I ought to.' Justin's expression was grim, the lines around his jaw tight and hard as a fist as he lowered himself on to the arm of a nearby chair. But when he spoke his tone was calm and clear.

'I ended my relationship with Eunice two months ago. It was an easy decision. One I should have made a long time ago. Eunice and I were never meant for each other. But she refused to accept it at first; she made a terrible fuss and I'm sure it was she who started the rumour about the imminent marriage. She was trying to compromise me, hoping I'd change my mind.'

Tina's breathing was measured as she sought to keep control of herself. She said in a stiff voice, through lips that felt like cardboard, 'You can't really blame her for being upset. After all, you were together for rather a long time.'

'Yes, we were. And that was why I decided to be patient and give her time to finally accept that it was over. I felt I at least owed her that.'

Then his expression suddenly hardened. 'But last night she went too far. That scene with you was inexcusable. There was no way I could tolerate that sort of behaviour.'

He had acted because of her. Tina felt a giddy thrust of pleasure.

'So it really is over?' She was starting to believe him now and it was terrifying, the sense of exhilaration she felt.

But Justin's expression was still grim. 'Yes, it finally is over. At approximately four o'clock this morning she packed her things and went back to London, vowing that I would never set eyes on her again. Though I can't say that greatly distresses me,' he added, his lips twisting, 'after some of the things that were revealed during last night's little ding-dong.'

So, that was why he looked tired. He'd been fighting all night with Eunice. Tina could think of fewer less pleasant ways of passing a night.

But before she could offer her commiserations he was leaning towards her, that grim, dark expression still clouding his face. 'A lot came out of last night's little discussion.' He paused, then continued, 'But the most important thing I learned was that I owe you a huge apology.'

'An apology? To me?' Tina was baffled. She smiled at him, puzzled, bewildered, strangely happy. 'Why do you owe me an apology?'

Was he going to apologise for last night? she wondered. That was scarcely necessary now. Not after all the things he'd just told her.

But that wasn't it at all. He reached out and took her hand. 'I have to apologise,' he told her, 'for something that happened a long time ago.'

'A long time ago?'

Tina's stomach was suddenly churning. The warm touch of him and that intense look in his eyes were tearing her apart, laying waste her senses. He was going to apologise for ever betraying her, she thought in a kind of delirium. He regretted their breaking up. He knew he should never have gone with Eunice.

Her heart was soaring. Everything was finally going to come right again. His feelings for her, like her feelings for him, had never changed, after all.

She waited for him to speak, scarcely daring to breathe.

Justin looked down at her hand, which he held in his, for a moment. Then, slowly, he raised his eyes to hers again. 'It's a misunderstanding that, although it dates from several years ago, has badly affected our recent dealings. It's created a friction between us that need never have been.'

Tina frowned curiously, her heart faltering a little. 'What do you mean?'

'It concerns your move to *Scope*.' Justin paused and sighed deeply. Then he continued, 'The circumstances surrounding that move were not, I have now discovered, as I was led to believe.'

Tina's heart had frozen a little. This was not what she'd been expecting. But perhaps he would come to that part later. She focused on what he'd just said and acknowledged that she already knew that. At least, she knew he'd been unaware that Eunice had fired her. But what difference could that have possibly made to their present dealings?

Her brow puckered. 'Surely that's all water under the bridge?'

Justin was shaking his head. 'No,' he said. His long fingers around her hand tightened a little. 'I'm afraid I've done you a great injustice.'

He was talking in riddles. 'I've no idea what you mean.'

'I know you don't.' A look of contrition touched his eyes. 'But the truth is I've misjudged you all these years.' He took a deep breath, as though what he was about to say pained him. Then, continuing to hold her hand tightly, he proceeded to explain.

'I was told that when you moved to *Scope* you betrayed *Miranda*. That in fact you'd been betraying it for months beforehand. Only last night did I discover that wasn't true at all.'

He had lost Tina totally. 'Betrayed *Miranda*? In what way?'

'I was told that for a long time before you handed in your notice you'd secretly been working on the pilot issue of *Scope*. That you stole ideas from *Miranda* and passed them on to *Scope*. That you betrayed JM Publications totally.'

Tina stared at him, stunned. 'But that's a total lie. Where could such a story have come from?'

Justin took another deep breath. 'I'm afraid it came from Eunice. At the time she even offered me so-called proof. And, fool that I was, I'm afraid I believed her.' He squeezed Tina's hand. 'But last night she revealed everything; she admitted it was all lies, that there wasn't a grain of truth in it, and

I want to apologise to you for ever having believed it. I realise now I've been grossly unfair to you.'

Tina's cheeks had gone quite pale. She sat up stiffly in her chair. 'Unfair, you say. It was more than unfair.' Suddenly, she wanted to snatch her hand away, but though she tried Justin was holding on to it too tightly. 'How could you have believed such a terrible thing?'

'It was wrong, I know. But the evidence was so convincing.' His face was filled with mingled contrition and anger. 'I can assure you, Eunice went to a great deal of trouble.'

'I'll bet she did.' Suddenly, Tina was remembering that nasty confrontation in Eunice's office all those years ago. Justin's story added up. Eunice had been out for her blood. But then she also remembered another confrontation. Her own with Justin at Charing Cross Station. The things she'd said then must merely have helped to convince him that every black word of Eunice's story was true.

He was saying now, looking into her eyes, his expression earnest, 'I can't begin to tell you how badly I feel about this. That incident has poisoned things between us. All these years I've believed those vile lies were true.'

Now something else was clicking into place in Tina's brain. She frowned at Justin. 'That was why you kept accusing me of having no loyalty, of only being out for what I could get.' Her eyes widened in hurt horror as another penny dropped. 'Did you also believe I might betray *Scope*? Is that why you were so scathing about my attempts to negotiate?'

'Yes, I'm afraid it was.' At least he did not deny it, though Tina could see that he found the admission hard. With a frown he reached up and softly touched her cheek. 'I'm really sorry, Tina. Please forgive me.'

At first Tina had felt anger, but now, unexpectedly, she felt moved. He was sorry. He did regret it. She could see it in his eyes. She glanced down at the hand that felt so warm against her skin and to her surprise she suddenly felt very close to him.

'Well, I'm glad you found out the truth.' She glanced up at him forgivingly. 'That was rather a dreadful thing to believe of anyone. No wonder your opinion of me was so low.'

'I should have known better.' He squeezed her hand tightly again. 'Last night when I found out I was sick to my soul.'

He watched her for a moment, seeing the forgiveness in her eyes, and some of the fierce intensity in his face began to soften. He smiled a halfsmile. 'There's something else I have to tell you. This was another of Eunice's lies, though I misled you too...'

He sighed. 'I have no intention of merging *Scope* with *Miranda*. I never have had. It would be a crazy thing to do. Each of them has its own audience and its own place in the market. *Scope*'s staying—as are all of Berry's other publications—so your job's safe, and so are those of all your colleagues.'

Tina blinked at him. 'You mean that?'

'I mean it absolutely.' He smiled, this time something approaching a real smile. 'I'll tell you something else. Since you're doing such a wonderful job as acting editor, when Maggie eventually retires you'll be first in line for her job.'

Tina frowned at him. 'You're not just saying that to make amends? Because, as much as I want that job, that's not the way I want to get it.'

'I know that.' He began to rise to his feet, gently but firmly drawing her with him. 'That's not why I would offer it.' He looked deep into her eyes. 'The only reason I would offer it to you is because you're the best one for the job.' He drew her towards him. 'I hope you believe me?'

Tina looked back at him and nodded. 'I believe you,' she answered. Her heart had suddenly flown to her throat.

'And you believe all the rest of what I've been telling you? About how badly I feel. About how this whole mess happened. And you forgive me? At least a little, I hope?'

Tina nodded again, not trusting herself to speak. For his arms were slipping round her, forming a circle around her waist, and the hardness of his chest was brushing against her breasts.

He kissed her nose. 'It's more than I deserve.'

She sighed. 'Perhaps it is.' Suddenly, she could not look at him. Her eyes were fixed somewhere in the region of his collarbone, concentrating on the sprinkling of fine black hairs there.

'I'll make it up to you. At least, I'll do my best.' Very softly, he bent down to kiss her on the cheek.

Tina could feel her heart quiver. It would be so easy for him to make it up to her. All he would have to do was show her he cared. If he did that, nothing else in the whole wide world would matter.

He was drawing her closer, so that his warmth was burning into her, and his hands were caressing her, playing her like piano keys, sending darts of excitement skittering down her spine.

Tina's hands were on his shoulders, moulding the firm, hard strength of him, her fingers reaching up to tangle with his hair. Heaven help me, she was thinking, every inch of him's so wonderful. How could I ever have believed for one moment that I didn't love him?

It was as though he was responding to these emotions in her. He drew back gently for a moment and looked long and deep into her eyes.

'We've wasted so much time,' he murmured, bending to kiss her earlobe. 'There's been so much bad blood between us, and all for nothing.' He frowned, his eyes as dark as infinity as they swept over her. 'What a pair of fools we are.'

Tina could feel her heart swell like a balloon inside her, and suddenly she had to tell him.

'Those things I told you at Charing Cross that day... All that crazy stuff about how I only used you... None of that was true,' she confessed.

He sighed and held her. 'Maybe in my heart I always knew it. But it's good to hear it. I've waited a long time.'

Then he pulled her against him, his mouth searching for hers. 'Oh, Tina! Oh, Tina!' His fingers were in her hair and all at once there was a passion in his kiss that scorched her, a fire that seemed to leap from him like some unleashed wild thing. Suddenly, it was Justin, the tiger, kissing her.

Tina shuddered with excitement and responded like a tigress, gasping and breathless from the power of his kisses, but eager and hungry and desperate for more.

She clung to him fiercely, her body pressed against him. And as his hand all at once reached inside her blouse, without preamble, unhooking her bra to free her breasts, her heart was thundering with a desire that was almost pain.

'Oh, please,' she breathed as his hand grazed her hard nipple. Take me, she was thinking. Make love to me right now.

Her blouse had come undone and Justin's shirt was all unbuttoned and she was standing there pressed up against him with her bra half off and her breasts exposed.

Justin bent down and caught one shamefully erect nipple between his lips. 'You're beautiful,' he murmured. 'Quite as beautiful as I remembered.'

Then, as she gasped and shuddered helplessly, he cupped both breasts in his hands. 'Shall we go upstairs and do this properly?'

It was all Tina could do not to cry out, Oh, yes, please! She nodded instead and swallowed hard. Suddenly, she felt as nervous and excited as a virgin. The way she had been with him three long years ago.

A shaft of desire shot through her as she looked up into his face. He was her first and only lover, and soon she would be his again. And she would surrender to him even more joyfully, even more passionately than before.

They were halfway across the room when the phone suddenly started ringing. It was terrible timing, for the phone was right in front of them. Another few steps and they would have been past it and probably Justin would have decided to ignore it. Instead, automatically, he picked it up and said hello.

A moment later Tina knew the party was over. Barely looking at her, Justin was holding the receiver out to her, while with his free hand he was carefully buttoning up his shirt.

'It's for you,' he said, his voice as hard as gravel. 'It's the boyfriend. Mike.'

CHAPTER NINE

LATER, back in London, once she had recovered her senses, Tina decided that that phone call had been a very good thing. It had quenched, just as thoroughly as a bucket of cold water, a highly flammable situation. And the timing had been perfect. Just a few seconds later and, without a doubt, she'd have ended up in bed with Justin.

At the time, of course, her reaction had been rather different. As he'd walked away from her, buttoning up his shirt, without even a glance at her, his expression shuttered, she'd felt as though the ground had opened up beneath her feet. Suddenly, she was crashing from the dizzy heights of anticipation into a vast dark hole of nothingness. One moment there'd been magic all around her, the next a rush of cold rejection. She'd felt so shocked, so disappointed, she'd almost burst into tears.

But she hadn't. She'd taken the phone. 'Hello? Mike?' she'd queried, wondering why on earth he could possibly be phoning her, wondering how he'd even known where she was.

She'd had her answer to both questions almost immediately.

'Are you all right? I got an urgent message to ring you on this number. Where are you? What's going on?' he'd wanted to know.

An urgent message. Even in her dazed state, Tina had put two and two together. The urgent message no doubt had come, anonymously, from Eunice. This was her final, spiteful act of revenge. A bid to stir up trouble between Justin and Tina.

'I'm fine,' Tina had assured Mike, hurriedly refastening her blouse and stuffing it back inside the waistband of her skirt. 'There's nothing to worry about. I'll speak to you later.'

Then, as she'd laid down the phone, she'd turned to Justin. 'That was Mike. He just wanted to say hello.'

She could have told him the truth, of course, but sanity was already dawning, and it was much better to let him go on believing what he believed. For any further intimacy between them, Tina was realising, would be madness. Divine madness, undoubtedly. But madness all the same. Had she forgotten how badly he had treated her three years ago? What was to stop him doing the same again?

And so, less than fifteen minutes later, she'd been driving away from Beech Hedges and heading towards the motorway to London, vowing to put this weekend behind her and to return to the previous simple order of her life. *Scope*'s future was safe, after all, and that was what mattered. Everything else was simply excess baggage.

But it was a heavy load to carry, as she found out over the following week. All sorts of new feelings had been awakened inside her. All sorts of desires. All sorts of dreams.

It seemed she thought of Justin from the moment she woke up until, exhausted, she finally fell asleep again at night. And she didn't just think of him. She yearned for him, unbearably. She yearned for his touch, for his kisses, for the taste of him. Her heart felt as though it was breaking up inside her.

She hadn't seen him all week. There was that to be thankful for. To see him would only have added to her torment. The word was he'd gone up north—now that the take-over of Berry's had gone through—to size up another publication he had his eye on. One thing was for sure. He wasn't thinking of her.

And she must stop thinking of him. She must cut him from her mind. That was the task she had set herself for the weekend. For, if she continued the way she was going, she'd drive herself crazy. The human heart, after all, could only take so much pain.

The best way to sort herself out, she'd decided, was on her own, so she'd turned down her chief sub Vicki's invitation for Saturday lunchtime.

'Mike and I have got a job on Saturday,' she'd told Tina. 'We'll be going to the pub afterwards. Why don't you join us?'

Tina had shaken her head. 'No, thanks, Vicki. I've got a thousand things to do. I'll take a rain check.'

Some other weekend, she was thinking, once she'd managed to get her head straight. Besides, it was certain that the conversation would turn to Justin. For everyone was talking about the break-up of his engagement and Eunice's sudden departure for some top job in New York.

It was all good news, but all the same it would be sheer torture to have to sit and listen to everyone discussing it.

So Tina spent Saturday on her own, keeping herself busy—shopping, washing the car, reorganising her wardrobe. And every time she thought of Justin she simply chased the thought away. She must learn, finally and forever, to stop thinking of him.

And she felt a great deal better for her day of activity. As she sat watching a video later that evening, she began making some similar plans for tomorrow.

She'd go for a drive. Nowhere in particular. Just to blow the cobwebs from her hair. Then in the evening she'd write some letters and phone her parents. It was going to be another therapeutic and productive day.

Tina clenched her fists determinedly. She would get over this misery. And for a moment, as she fixed on her determination, that cloudy dark look disappeared from her blue eyes and a spark of her old spirit glowed again. An observer at that moment would have been forgiven for believing that she had finally driven away all the demons that haunted her, and that that spot where hope lived no longer throbbed inside her, as empty and barren as a desert.

*   *   *

Tina awoke next morning feeling reassuringly positive.

She jumped out of bed before her mood could alter, pulled on jeans and a sweatshirt and hurried down to the corner shop to buy some milk and the Sunday papers. She'd have a leisurely breakfast reading the papers, then take the car and drive somewhere for lunch. It was a beautiful autumn day. She was going to enjoy it.

But Lenny, who ran the corner shop, was apologetic when she asked for her paper.

'I've got the paper all right, but the magazine's missing. I've phoned up and they should be arriving in about ten minutes.' He glanced at his young son Jim who helped him at weekends. 'I can get the young lad to deliver it when they arrive, if you like?'

Tina smiled at him gratefully. 'That would be perfect.' She winked at young Jim. 'I'll see you later, then.'

She crossed the sunny street with her pint of milk and papers, feeling her spirits lifting even higher. See how friendly everyone was! See how the sun was shining! What did she have to be miserable about?

Up in her first-floor flat she stepped into the sunny kitchen and laid her paper and milk on the kitchen table. Then she poured out some corn-flakes and a glass of orange juice from the fridge, sat down and spread the papers out before her. For the first time for a long time the ache inside her had softened. You see, she told herself, it pays to be positive!

She was halfway through her cornflakes when the doorbell rang. Tina smiled to herself. That would be Jim with her magazine. She darted through to the bedroom to take twenty pence from her bag. The little lad deserved a tip!

The doorbell rang again as she hurried out into the hall. 'I'm coming!' she called. Young Jim was obviously feeling impatient! She pulled the door open, smiling broadly. 'Thank you,' she began. Then she froze on the spot.

It was her magazine all right. The figure on the landing was holding it out to her.

'I believe this is yours.'

But it wasn't Jim. It was Justin.

For a moment Tina just stood there, utterly speechless, staring at the incongruous sight of Justin holding out her magazine. Then she found her voice at last. 'What are you doing here—with that?'

Justin glanced down for a moment at the magazine in his hand. 'I asked this kid I met downstairs which floor you lived on. He told me and said he was about to deliver this. So I gave him fifty pence and said I'd deliver it for him.' He smiled an odd smile. 'I hope you don't mind?'

Tina frankly wasn't sure whether she minded or not. She felt numb, confused, her pulses racing. He was standing there, dressed in dark trousers and a light shirt, looking like some bright star that had just dropped down from heaven. And though she was desperately trying not to feel pleased to see him her heart was crashing about with sheer delight inside her.

She said, not answering his question, 'But why are you here?'

'Just to say hello—and to bring you these.' As he spoke, he held out his other hand, which had been hidden behind his back, to reveal a bunch of deep red roses.

'Roses?'

Tina felt her cheeks turn the same colour as the petals. Suddenly, her knees felt like rubber beneath her. Was she dreaming this? Surely she must be. This couldn't be Justin come to bring her roses?

She looked at him, trying hard to hide her confusion. 'Why on earth would you bring me roses?'

He did not answer immediately. Then he said, quite softly, 'May I come in? I'd like to talk.'

Tina wanted to say no. Suddenly she felt deeply fearful of the emotions that were writhing about inside her. And the most terrifying of them all was hope.

But she could not say no. Stiffly, she stood aside, scarcely daring to breathe as he stepped past her into the hallway. The sudden scent of him in her nostrils made her dizzy.

As she stood there awkwardly, heart beating like a tom-tom, he paused and handed her the bunch of flowers. 'Here,' he said. 'You'd better put these in water.'

Tina grabbed them almost gratefully and headed blindly for the kitchen. Suddenly she felt as though she was trembling all over. This little task, if nothing else, would give her a moment to collect herself.

She laid the flowers on the draining-board and, feeling like a sleep-walker, bent to open the cupboard where she kept things like vases. She pulled one out at random, placed it in the sink and with numb, clumsy fingers turned on the cold tap.

'I see you were in the middle of breakfast. I'm sorry if I interrupted you.' Justin had followed her into the kitchen and was standing by the table, glancing down at the half-finished bowl of corn-flakes. 'But don't worry about me. Go ahead and finish eating.'

'No, I won't, thank you very much.' Tina turned to face him, her confusion suddenly turning to defensive irritation. What did he think he was doing turning up on her doorstep, then coming into her house and proceeding to order her about? Put the flowers in water. Finish your breakfast. Who the devil did he think he was?

She felt something snap inside her. She turned on him angrily. 'Stop telling me what to do! And what are you doing here anyway? Is this some kind of joke—bringing me roses!'

'Would you rather Mike had brought them?'

Something shifted in his eyes and stopped the, Perhaps I would! that was rising defensively to Tina's lips. Instead, she just looked back at him, not knowing what to think. What was going on? For something clearly was.

And then, suddenly, as she stood there, he was stepping towards her, causing Tina to dart aside and

let out a little cry of panic. If he tried to touch her,
she would fall apart. But he was simply reaching
past her to turn off the tap. 'The vase was over-
flowing,' he said with a small smile, looking into
her unhappy, startled face. Then, frowning, he
reached out and took hold of her hand. 'Tina, we've
got to talk. Let's go and sit down somewhere.'

Next moment he was propelling her towards the
door. 'I take it the sitting-room's through here?'

'What do you think you're doing?' Tina tried to
pull away from him. 'I don't want to sit and talk
to you!'

But he ignored her feeble protests and almost
carried her through to the sitting-room, seated her
in one of the armchairs and drew up the other one
to face her. Then, lowering himself in it, he took
hold of both her hands. He leaned towards her,
dark eyes serious, and told her. 'Hear me out, Tina.
That's all I ask of you. Just give me a couple of
minutes of your time.'

It wasn't her time Tina was worried about. It was
what was happening inside her. Her heart seemed
to be clattering in all directions. She didn't know
if she wanted to hear what he had to say. And yet,
at the same time, she knew she must.

She took a deep breath, closed her eyes and
waited.

'All of what I'm about to tell you is absolutely
true.'

When Justin began to speak his voice was low
and earnest, and there was a sense of poised stillness
in him, like someone holding their breath. Tina

sensed that what he was about to tell her he had longed to tell her for a long time. She opened her eyes, her heart as tight as a drum inside her, and watched him as he started to explain.

'Eunice and I were never really engaged. I never proposed to her. I never wanted us to marry. We had a relationship, but that was all.'

As Tina's mouth dropped open, about to protest her disbelief, he continued, not giving her a chance to speak. 'I know what people thought—but that was because of what Eunice told them. As you know, she's good at spreading rumours. I never denied them because, quite frankly, they suited me. But there was never any special understanding between the two of us.'

'What about the ring?'

Was that supposed to be a figment of her imagination? Did he really think he could fool her with this pack of nonsense?

'The ring was Eunice's. It had belonged to an aunt. She liked to pretend it was an engagement ring, but I can assure you it wasn't.'

Tina's brain was spinning. She still didn't believe him.

'You're lying to me again. I don't believe any of this. You're lying to me, just like you lied to me all the time we were together!' She tried to pull her hands free, her voice breaking with emotion. 'All the time you were seeing me you were secretly seeing Eunice! And then, behind my back, you went and got engaged to her!'

With sudden strength she managed to tear her hands free and staggered clumsily to her feet. 'You're a liar! All you've ever done is lie to me!'

'I've never lied to you, Tina.' As she tried to dart away from him, Justin jumped to his feet and caught hold of her firmly, pulling her towards him, dark eyes burning into her face. 'There was nothing going on between Eunice and me at that time. The only woman in my life was you.'

Tina stopped struggling for a moment at the urgency in his tone. Feeling her heart trip inside her, she looked up into his face. 'I don't believe you. You're lying,' she said again, weakly.

'I'm not lying, Tina. I've never lied to you.' As he spoke, Justin continued to hold her firmly. 'There was nothing going on between Eunice and me then. She only told you that to break us up.'

There was a tightness in his voice, strung out like piano wire. 'She lied to us both. We were both her victims. That night when she confessed her lies about you betraying *Miranda* she also admitted how she'd told you we were engaged when we weren't.' He gave her a small shake. 'But how could you have believed it? How could you have believed I'd been seeing Eunice behind your back? Didn't I show you how much I loved you?'

Tina's brain was suddenly spinning. Should she believe him or not? 'But you always kept our relationship so secret. If you loved me, why did you do that?'

'I didn't keep it secret. I was just trying to be discreet. At the time, I thought it was the right thing to do.' Justin shrugged a helpless shrug. 'I realise now I was wrong if it made you doubt for one moment that I loved you.'

'But *did* you love me? I mean *really* love me?' Tina was still having difficulty accepting what he was telling her. How could she have been wrong for all these years? 'If you'd really loved me, you could never have believed I'd betray *Miranda*.'

'I didn't believe it, not in the beginning. Though I have to confess I was wondering what was going on. At the time when all this happened I was over in the States and you'd behaved so strangely when I phoned you from Houston to tell you I was going to have to stay on another few weeks, banging down the phone and refusing to speak to me again, that I was already starting to think there was something a bit odd going on. Though when Eunice flew out to join me—strictly business—and started showing me all the so-called evidence against you, I refused to believe that it was true.'

Tina's cheeks had gone ashen. 'You phoned to tell me that? I thought you'd phoned me to tell me about the engagement.' She felt sick to her soul. She'd made a terrible mistake.

'You thought what?' Justin was staring at her in equal horror. 'You mean that's why you went crazy and finally hung up on me?' He closed his eyes for a moment with a painful shudder. 'This whole thing is a nightmare,' he muttered. Then he continued, 'I kept trying to phone you after that, but you'd changed your number. I couldn't get through. And then when I got back I discovered you'd even moved house. It was obvious you were determined to avoid me at all costs. But, even then, I kept trying for weeks to get hold of you, hoping you would tell me Eunice's stories weren't true.' His voice faltered. 'But instead, when I bumped into you at Charing Cross, the stuff you told me simply seemed to confirm her stories.' He shook her as his frustration and grief overwhelmed him. 'Those moments at Charing Cross Station were the worst moments of my life.'

Tina felt tears rise to her eyes at that look on his face. What a terrible, fatal thing she'd done.

She said in a small voice, 'Like I told you, it was all lies.'

He squeezed her hands. 'Yes, I know that now. I only wish I'd known it at the time.' He sighed. 'That was when I got involved with Eunice. It was a diversion. Nothing more. And for the most part it was pretty undemanding. When she's not being a bitch, Eunice can be a lot of fun.'

As Tina's gaze flickered, suddenly stung by a flash of jealousy, he bent to kiss her nose and added with a sombre smile, 'And most important, it suited me to be temporarily out of circulation. It gave me a chance to try and get over you.'

He drew her into his arms. 'Oh, Tina. My Tina.' He held her close for a moment and kissed her hair. 'If only we'd had a little more faith in each other's love.'

Then he seemed to hold his breath as he drew away a little to look at her. 'You did love me, didn't you? I'm not wrong about that?'

There were tears in Tina's eyes. She could no longer hold them back. As she looked into his face and blinked, the tears rolled down her cheeks. But behind the tears her eyes were smiling.

'Oh, yes, I loved you. With all my heart I loved you. Losing you was the greatest sorrow of my life.'

'And losing you was mine. It still is,' he told her. He bent to kiss away the salty tears on her cheeks. 'I love you, Tina. I've never stopped loving you. Please tell me I haven't lost you completely after all.'

Tina looked into his eyes that shone down like pools of magic and felt her heart turn over with pure joy. For all at once all the sadness inside her had vanished. The past and all its regrets no longer mattered. The only thing that mattered was now. This minute.

She flung her arms round him. 'You could never lose me! Never! Never! I'll always be yours!'

And as he hugged her and held her and swept her off her feet, she just had time to add as his lips crushed down on hers, 'Don't you know you're the only man I've ever loved in my whole life?'

'So, how are we going to thank Mike and Vicki?'

Justin bent to kiss the face that looked up at him dreamily from the pillow. 'If it weren't for them, we wouldn't be here now.'

'In that case, I think we should give them both a medal.' Tina smiled and stretched languorously beneath the cool cotton sheet, her hands lovingly caressing Justin's naked torso. 'For there's nowhere in the whole world I'd rather be,' she told him, reaching up to plant a kiss on his suntanned shoulder. 'And no one in the whole world I'd rather be with.'

For, after declaring his love, Justin had carried her through to the bedroom and laid her gently on the big double bed. And there, after three long years spent longing for one another, finally, spectacularly, they'd come together. Neither of them would ever forget that wonderful act of love.

Afterwards, for a while, they had lain quietly together, warm bodies entwined, caressing one another, blissfully breathing in each other's scents. And it had seemed to Tina that she had never known such happiness. It spread through her like warm honey and filled her to the brim.

She looked at Justin now, her eyes bright with love for him. 'I really mean what I said about the medals,' she told him. 'I feel I owe my life to Mike and Vicki.' She held on to Justin tightly for a moment and kissed him. It scared her to think how if it hadn't been for her two friends this wonderful moment might never have been. For Justin had told her about yesterday's chance meeting with Mike and Vicki.

'Luckily,' he'd recounted, 'I'd decided to spend the weekend in London and I bumped into them when I dropped into a pub in the West End at lunchtime. Apparently, they'd just been out on a job together. I don't know Vicki, but I know Mike by sight and we said hello and exchanged a few words.'

Tina had heard the details before, but she asked him now, 'Tell me again what happened when you bumped into them?'

Justin smiled. 'Well, on an impulse, I asked him, How's the girlfriend? He looked at me a little strangely. "What girlfriend?" he asked. Tina, I said. Then Vicki butted in. "Tina's not Mike's girlfriend," she informed me.'

He scowled at Tina mock-angrily now and for the umpteenth time demanded, 'Why did you tell me Mike was your boyfriend? If I hadn't thought that, I'd have told you all about Eunice and me ages ago. I wasn't telling anyone else, but for you I'd have made an exception. I actually thought seriously about doing it at one point. But then I decided against it. I thought there was no point, since you'd said you were involved with Mike.'

Tina scowled back at him. 'Mike was my protection against you. I was trying to keep you at a distance.'

Then she shivered inwardly. I was mad, she told herself. I was keeping him at such a safe distance I very nearly lost him! Thank heavens for Vicki and Mike in the pub!

Justin caught a lock of her hair and tugged it gently, as though to punish her for her misdemeanour. 'I don't know about keeping me at a distance,' he told her, 'but you certainly succeeded in making me jealous.'

'Jealous? Were you really jealous?'

'Disgustingly jealous. I couldn't bear to think of another man making love to you.'

'I'm pleased to hear it.' Tina reached up and kissed him. 'If I'd known that,' she teased, 'I'd have laid it on even thicker.'

'Any thicker and poor old Mike mightn't have lived to tell the tale.' Justin laughed and took hold of her and nibbled her earlobe. Then he pulled her to him and kissed her on the lips, his fingers caressing her naked breast as he did so.

'I've got a better idea than medals,' he murmured. 'I can think of a much more appropriate way to thank them.'

'How?' Tina shivered and curled more closely against him. Every time he touched her she melted inside. 'How do you think we should thank them? Tell me.'

Justin shifted slightly. 'First, let me remind you that there's someone else we ought to thank.' He kissed her earlobe again. 'The security man at JM. The guy who let you in to see me in the first place. If he hadn't, we might never even have got to first base.'

Tina smiled and glanced up at him. 'You didn't sack him, did you?' She knew he hadn't. She'd already checked that out. She kissed him. 'So, how do you think we should thank them all?'

Justin paused for just an instant, then he took hold of her chin lightly and let his gaze pour down over her for a moment. Then he kissed her again and, very softly, told her, 'I think we should invite them to be guests of honour at our wedding.'

'Wedding?'

Tina blinked. Her heart stopped with a thud.

Justin smiled at her. 'There is going to be a wedding, I hope?'

Tina blinked again and nodded. 'If you insist.'

'I do. Absolutely. And there's something else I insist on.' Justin kissed her nose. 'It's going to be announced in all the papers. Never again will you be able to accuse me of keeping you a secret. This time, I promise you, the whole world's going to know.'

Tina felt dizzy with happiness. She reached up and hugged him. 'Have I ever told you how much I love you?' she demanded, kissing him.

'Not nearly often enough.' Justin pulled her close to him and held her tightly for a moment. 'And I haven't told you nearly often enough either. But I'm going to make up for that. You're going to get tired of hearing it.'

As Tina shook her head, knowing that was impossible—she could never get tired of hearing him say he loved her—he took hold of her hand and raised it to his lips.

'I warn you, this wedding is going to happen very soon. I've already waited for you more than long enough. So, this evening you and I are going to have dinner somewhere special and start making some serious plans for the future.'

And that, after another bout of love, was precisely what happened. That evening they had dinner at their favourite restaurant near Chatham, the one they used to go to regularly in the old days. And over champagne they fixed their wedding date for early December. 'Two months,' Justin told her, 'is as long as I can wait.' And though Tina had been right, she'd never tire of hearing him say he loved her, as the evening wore on she was growing deliciously used to hearing it.

Still, as she looked into his eyes across the candlelit table, she had to ask him, 'Tell me one more time.'

Justin laid down his glass. 'I love you,' he told her, smiling.

And at that moment, right on cue, the resident parrot—who hadn't forgotten any of his old tricks in the meantime—let out a deafening whistle of approval!

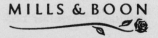

MILLS & BOON

CHRISTMAS CRACKERS

*A cracker of a gift pack full of
Mills & Boon goodies. You'll find...*

Passion—in *A Savage Betrayal* by Lynne Graham

A beautiful baby—in *A Baby for Christmas* by Anne McAllister

A Yuletide wedding—in *Yuletide Bride* by Mary Lyons

A Christmas reunion—in *Christmas Angel* by Shannon Waverly

Special Christmas price of 4 books
for £5.99 (usual price £7.96)

Published: November 1995

*Available from WH Smith, John Menzies, Volume One, Forbuoys, Martins,
Tesco, Asda, Safeway and other paperback stockists.*

MILLS & BOON

By Request

*Bestselling romances brought
back to you by popular demand*

Two complete novels in one volume
by bestselling author

Robyn Donald

Storm over Paradise
The Stone Princess

Available: November 1995   Price: £3.99

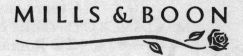

MILLS & BOON

Next Month's Romances

Each month you can choose from a wide variety of romance with Mills & Boon. Below are the new titles to look out for next month.

A WEDDING TO REMEMBER	Emma Darcy
A WOMAN OF PASSION	Anne Mather
FATE TAKES A HAND	Betty Neels
CALUM	Sally Wentworth
BEYOND REACH	Sandra Field
AN OBSESSIVE LOVE	Sarah Holland
THE SECRET BABY	Day Leclaire
NO HOLDING BACK	Kate Walker
MAKE-BELIEVE MARRIAGE	Renee Roszel
TOMORROW'S BRIDE	Alexandra Scott
BETWEEN MIST AND MIDNIGHT	Kathleen O'Brien
THE BLACK SHEEP	Susan Fox
PRISONER OF THE HEART	Liz Fielding
AN AMBITIOUS HEART	Marjorie Lewty
TO LOVE AND PROTECT	Kate Denton
THE MOON LADY'S LOVER	Vanessa Grant

A years supply of Mills & Boon Romances — absolutely free!

Would you like to win a years supply of heartwarming and passionate romances? Well, you can and they're FREE! All you have to do is complete the wordsearch puzzle below and send it to us by 30th April 1996. The first 5 correct entries picked after that date will win a years supply of Mills & Boon Romance novels (six books every month — worth over £100). What could be easier?

STOCKHOLM	PARIS	HELSINKI	ANKARA
REYKJAVIK	LONDON	ROME	AMSTERDAM
COPENHAGEN	PRAGUE	VIENNA	OSLO
MADRID	ATHENS	LIMA	

N	O	L	S	O	P	A	R	I	S
E	Q	U	V	A	F	R	O	K	T
G	C	L	I	M	A	A	M	N	O
A	T	H	E	N	S	K	E	I	C
H	L	O	N	D	O	N	H	S	K
N	S	H	N	R	I	A	O	L	H
E	D	M	A	D	R	I	D	E	O
P	R	A	G	U	E	U	Y	H	L
O	A	M	S	T	E	R	D	A	M
C	R	E	Y	K	J	A	V	I	K

Please turn over for details on how to enter ➡

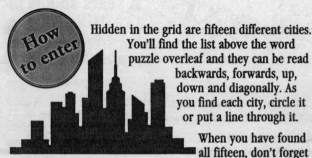

How to enter

Hidden in the grid are fifteen different cities. You'll find the list above the word puzzle overleaf and they can be read backwards, forwards, up, down and diagonally. As you find each city, circle it or put a line through it.

When you have found all fifteen, don't forget to fill in your name and address in the space provided below and pop this page in an envelope (you don't need a stamp) and post it today. Hurry – competition ends 30th April 1996.

Mills & Boon Capital Wordsearch
FREEPOST
Croydon
Surrey
CR9 3WZ

Are you a Reader Service Subscriber?   Yes ❑   No ❑

Ms/Mrs/Miss/Mr _____

Address _____

_____

_____ Postcode _____

One application per household.

You may be mailed with other offers from other reputable companies as a result of this application. If you would prefer not to receive such offers, please tick box.   ❑   COMP495
                                                                                                      D